CLUB TIMES

For Members' Eyes Only

Smooth Operator on the Loose!

While I checked out some vehicles at the used car lot of Lone Star County, my ears perked up at the sound of sweet words. When I looked up, I was staring at the newest hotshot of Mission Creek—Ace Turner Carson—and he'd coated me with a thick layer of honey. Ladies, I'm warning you, this man is lethally charming. Because I'm a sharp woman of a certain sophistication (stop laughing, Ford), I knew Ace was just talkin' purdy.

Change of topic, isn't that Crystal Bennett as sweet as can be? She's done such a bang-up job on the ribbon-cutting ceremony for the new maternity wing at Mission Creek Memorial. Of course, I care more about whether or not her red hair is real. While we shared a brioche in the Yellow Rose Café, I asked her if she dyed her hair. Crystal giggled and said, "Don't be silly."

(In LSCC-speak, this means "drop dead.")

Having received hot and cold reactions from Ace and Crystal this week, I'm ready for a Jacuzzi with some of Lone Star's finest (as long as I don't have to see them in their swimwear). Why don't you come along with us and cool off at the Lone Star Country Club!

P9-DWW-222

About the Author

MYRNA MACKENZIE,

married to her high school sweetheart, with two (very tall and always hungry) teenage sons, has been blessed by the joys of family. She's had the chance to be a teacher and to learn all the cool things that kids can teach us about human nature. She's traveled, hiked mountains, rafted white water and seen bear and elk up close. And, since 1993, when she began writing for Silhouette, she's also had the privilege of being able to share the stories she loves to write with readers around the world. Winner of the Holt Medallion honoring outstanding literary talent, and a finalist in the Readers' Choice Awards and the Orange Rose contest, Myrna likes to think of herself as a professional (but hardworking) daydreamer.

Myrna was thrilled when she was asked to be part of the LONE STAR COUNTRY CLUB continuity. The opportunity to work with some of her favorite authors, to be a part of such an exciting and complex story and to have the chance to flesh out characters who were so much fun to work with has been a joy. You can contact Myrna by writing to her at P.O. Box 225, LaGrange, Illinois 60525 or by visiting her Web site at www.myrnamackenzie.com.

MYRNA MACKENZIE

HER SWEET TALKIN' MAN

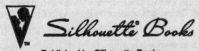

Published by Silhouette Books
America's Publisher of Contemporary Romance

Special thanks and acknowledgment are given to Myrna Mackenzie for her contribution to the LONE STAR COUNTRY CLUB series.

SILHOUETTE BOOKS

ISBN 0-373-61364-4

HER SWEET TALKIN' MAN

Copyright © 2002 by Harlequin Books S.A.

This edition published by arrangement with Harlequin Books S.A.

® and TM are trademarks of Harlequin Books S.A., used under license. Trademarks indicated with ® are registered in the United States Patent and Trademark Office, the Canadian Trade Marks Office and in other countries.

Visit Silhouette at www.eHarlequin.com

Printed in U.S.A.

THE FAMILIES

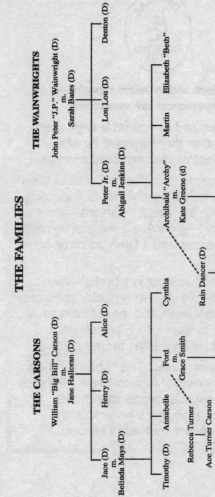

THE CARSONS

William "Big Bill" Carson (D)
m.
Jane Halloran (D)

Jace (D)   Henry (D)   Alice (D)
m.   m.
Belinda Mays (D)

Timothy (D)   Annabelle   Ford   Cynthia
                   m.
        Rebecca Turner   Grace Smith

Ace Turner Carson

Flynt   Matt   Cara   Fiona

THE WAINWRIGHTS

John Peter "J.P." Wainwright (D)
m.
Sarah Bates (D)

Peter Jr. (D)   Lou Lou (D)   Denton (D)
m.
Abigail Jenkins (D)

Archibald "Archy"   Martin   Elizabeth "Beth"
m.
Kate Greene (d)

Justin   Rose   Susan

Rain Dancer (D)

Hawk

D   Deceased
d   Divorced
m.   Married
----   Affair
——   Twins

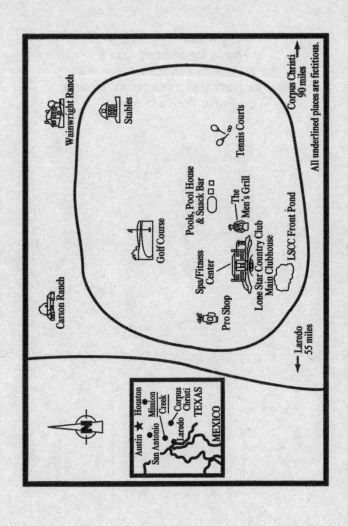

Wainwright Ranch

Carson Ranch

Stables

Golf Course

Pools, Pool House & Snack Bar

Spa/Fitness Center

Pro Shop

The Men's Grill

Lone Star Country Club Main Clubhouse

Tennis Courts

LSCC Front Pond

← Laredo 55 miles

Corpus Christi 90 miles →

All underlined places are fictitious.

Austin ★ Houston
San Antonio
Mission Creek
Laredo Corpus Christi
TEXAS
MEXICO

N

To my sister-in-law, Pat—
Thanks for umpteen favors,
for making my brother a happy man
and for hosting all those holiday dinners.
You've been a blessing.

One

"Whoa, this is going to be some family reunion. Especially since the rest of the family doesn't even know I exist," Ace Turner Carson said to himself as he pulled his white sedan into the above-ground parking garage of the Mission Creek Memorial Hospital.

No surprise, though, since he himself hadn't even known his true roots until three months ago when his mother died.

But now he knew. Something he almost wished he didn't know, he thought with a grimace. And he'd had to take the next step and come to Mission Creek, Texas. His mother had suffered years of humiliation and pain after she'd been abandoned by the man she loved. Ford Carson deserved to suffer a little humiliation in kind.

Who better to engineer that than a hell-raising bad seed of an unwanted son?

"So bring on the family reunion," Ace whispered. "And let's make it as public an event as possible. Past time to get in the dance, buddy."

Besides, Ace had to admit, this could be fun—in spite of all his misgivings about being here in this unfamiliar town where the wealthy Carsons had so much influence, in spite of his reluctance even to meet

the man who had given him life. He smiled. Could
be real fun. Especially if he hammed things up a bit
and worked hard at being an embarrassment to his
dear old dad.

"Oh, yes, this is going to involve some intense
concentration, Carson. Some single-minded devo-
tion."

Which was why when he saw a petite, well-curved
redhead making a beeline for the parking-garage elevator, which was where he was headed, Ace ignored
his automatic response to her undeniably appealing
body.

"No distractions," he reminded himself. "You
came here for a reason."

Yes, but that didn't mean he'd gone completely
numb to the world and blind to the things that made
a man a man and a woman a woman. He might be
on a single-minded quest, but this was no ordinary
woman. And, after all, he wasn't going to do anything
but look, anyway. And maybe flirt—just a bit. An
elevator ride didn't leave a man time for much more.

As she drew nearer and scanned her surroundings,
clearly on the alert for thugs and wolves on the prowl,
he noted her wide hazel eyes, which held a hint of
innocence in spite of the fact that she appeared to be
in her early thirties. Interesting. What was even more
interesting was that below the hemline of her knee-
length ice-blue suit was a pair of the finest legs ever
to grace Texas, or even the planet. Her hair was a
mass of silk held back with silver clips. The strands
practically begged for a man to unsnap those clips
and sift through the silk with his fingertips.

Of course, touching her was absolutely out of the question. He wanted to admire her, not distress her. So when an elderly couple turned down the aisle on their way to the elevator, too, Ace grinned at them and moved forward. The red-haired beauty would know she was safe now.

He sauntered toward the elevator, his long legs taking him there ahead of her.

"Allow me to get that for you, darlin'" he said, stepping forward to push the elevator button. "Looks like your hands are full."

The lady stopped in her tracks. She had reached out for the button at the same moment he had, and she looked down at his hand, which was just over her own. Her skin nearly met his. He could feel her warmth. He could feel something else radiating from her. Awareness?

"Thank you, sir," she said. "But I think you're mistaken about my inability to handle such a simple task. After all, my hands aren't nearly full. I'm only carrying a clipboard. And I'm truly sorry, but I don't *ever* answer to the name darlin'."

He raised a brow because, after all, she *had* just answered.

A slight blush turned her cheeks an endearing rose as she realized her mistake. And did he say that her eyes held a trace of innocence? Well, yes, they did, but they could also flash intense green sparks when she was perturbed. And she appeared to be pretty darn perturbed right now.

Ace couldn't help smiling at the thought—and he couldn't help being intrigued. That blush and those eyes told him she hadn't had much experience with men like him, who blatantly spoke their minds or didn't bother hiding their interest. But she didn't back away. Her hair swung back when she dared to look up and stare him straight into his eyes. That was fortunate for him, since the movement exposed a neck that was long and pretty and pale. It made him dream of nibbling that tender spot just beneath her ear to see if he could make her sigh and gasp.

His entire body responded to the thought, an overly intense reaction that gave him pause.

Careful, buddy, he warned himself. Easy. She hadn't revealed her skin on purpose and would no doubt be appalled if she knew that the neat little collar of her suit made him think of peeling back the lapels and letting his fingers brush her flesh. She was obviously a by-the-book, never-break-the-rules kind of lady and he was a prowling alley cat, a man who never, ever touched a woman who hadn't been born a little wild and who liked things that way. Seeing how *she* was, however, he should probably just apologize and call the game off.

"You're right. I misspoke. Excuse me," he said as the elderly couple and the elevator arrived and he motioned everyone in ahead of him with a slight bow. But then he stepped in behind the redhead, and the orange-blossom scent of her slipped in and caught him unawares. Nothing like the enticing scent of a lovely woman to play havoc with a man's good intentions.

He moved in just a touch closer to her than was

proper. "I'll let you push *this* button if it makes you feel better," he murmured, gazing into her eyes.

Those eyes blinked. "Excuse me?" She turned a delicious shade of pink.

The old man chuckled. His wife smiled but shook her head at Ace as if to reprimand him for his manners.

"I need to get off at the main floor, darlin'," he directed, his lips twitching as he tried to hold back his smile. His hazel-eyed lady was clearly struggling to prove to the world that she was terribly sophisticated and dignified. He wouldn't spoil her illusions and announce that he'd seen she was still untutored in the ways of the wild.

Anyone could see that, he thought as she pushed the button for him and then one for the other couple. That prim little telltale voice might have been silent as the elevator descended, but when the doors opened at the next floor and the elderly couple exited, his lady clearly showed signs of common sense and a healthy dose of wariness. She moved to the corner and glanced up at him nervously.

Instantly Ace felt ashamed to know that he was the cause of her fear. He'd teased her earlier because he'd wanted to see what happened to her eyes when her emotions ran away with her. Still, frightening or hurting a woman in any way was just about the lowest thing a man could do.

He stepped away, leaned back against the corner farthest from her and crossed his arms to show her that he wasn't going to grab her. "You were right to correct my bad manners," he said. "I apologize.

We're strangers, and you're smart not to have anything to do with anyone you haven't been properly introduced to.''

Who in hell in Mission Creek, Texas, would introduce him to anyone? No one knew who he was.

Once they did discover his identity and what kind of man he really was, they sure as Satan weren't going to welcome him, much less begin introducing him to the women of the community.

The redheaded beauty looked suddenly chagrinned.

''I'm sorry,'' she said. ''You're probably here for the ribbon-cutting ceremony for the new maternity ward. You're a guest, and you should be treated as such.''

She didn't look any more at ease with him than she had, but he finally realized that she was wearing some sort of hospital badge. She worked here and felt she had to put up with whatever he dished out. Now that she'd decided he had a legitimate reason for being here, she felt that she had to be kind to him, even to apologize when he had been in the wrong. Sudden fierce anger surged through Ace. Anger at himself for putting her in a position where she felt she had to be gracious to a man who had obviously invaded her comfort zone. Ironic. He knew better than anyone that women often bore the brunt of men's mistakes, yet here he was making a mistake and dumping the blame on his lovely victim. Hell, he was the one in the wrong. He *was* here for the ribbon-cutting ceremony, but his intentions were anything but innocent.

He shook his head and held up one hand to stop her from humbling herself before him any more.

"Ma'am," he said, dredging up a trace of charm and humor to at least try to put her at ease. "You were right not to want to talk to me. I've got a reputation as a flirt and an opportunistic rover. And a woman these days can never be too careful. Just keep doing what you're doing. It's the smartest way to be."

There. He could almost feel her relaxing.

For some reason that didn't make him feel good, because he realized that his words were true. A woman couldn't be too careful. If a man could put her at ease just with a few well-chosen words, then some no-good tomcat could take advantage of her, catch her off guard. But...well, heck, he couldn't be the guardian of the world. He wasn't even going to be in Mission Creek that long. Just long enough to kick up some dust, leave an impression and settle an old score. This woman, whoever she was, probably had a husband who could look after her. Besides, this slowpoke of an elevator was almost to the right floor, the main level.

Ace stood straighter, readying himself to get off and meet whatever was to come in the next few hours.

He stared up at the numbers on the digital readout.

Nothing happened.

Silence settled over the car.

The woman looked up anxiously at the numbers, which still didn't appear to be doing anything.

And then the silence seemed to get deeper. The soft creaking of the car ceased entirely. The lights flickered and then held.

But the car didn't buck up and continue on its way. There were no sounds of movement. There was just a lot of quiet and waiting. In the void of anything else, Ace could hear the beauty's breathing. He looked at her and saw her body stiffen. She stared up at the floor numbers as if willing them to move.

"I...I think we may be stuck." Her soft voice trembled slightly. She pushed the button for the floor, then pushed it again. And again.

Nothing happened.

"Oh, no." She turned frightened eyes to Ace. She licked her lips nervously. All her cool facade of moments before drained away. "I...I think..." she began, and then stopped as if her mind was a jumble, as if she was too terrified to speak.

"Shh," he whispered. "It's all right. I'm sure things will get moving soon." Although he didn't know anything of the sort.

No matter. Those big hazel eyes were pools of lost hopes. Her clipboard slid to the floor, and her small hands curled into tight fists.

"I'm...I'm sure you're right," she managed to get out, but her teeth chattered in spite of the fact that it was July in Texas and the air-conditioning seemed to have gone out with the power.

Ace took one look at the woe in her face, the way she was struggling to control herself in front of him when she was clearly terrified, and he wanted to take the elevator apart for her, to bodily move the car to the right floor.

"Let's just try the emergency phone," he said, dropping his voice to a low soothing tone as he reached for the receiver. Calmly he explained to the security officer who answered that he and another passenger were caught between floors.

"He's going to get the technicians," Ace told the woman when he hung up.

She almost visibly took control of herself. Her pretty lips tightening, she took a deep breath, squared her shoulders and gave a quick nod. "Okay," she said faintly. "That's very good."

But her eyes were just a touch too wide. Ace thought he still detected a faint tremble in her voice.

"We'll be out of here in no time, sunshine." He flashed her a reassuring smile. "Or am I not allowed to call you sunshine?"

Something that might have been a smile in other circumstances eased some of the tension around her lips. "I'm really sorry to be acting like such a fool." Her soft red curls slid against her cheeks as she shook her head. "It's rather embarrassing to admit but…I'm afraid I'm not very good in small spaces. At least not when I'm stuck in one."

He wanted to ask why. Had something happened in her past that had brought on these feelings of claustrophobia? But then, he was touchy about his own past. He certainly didn't ask others about theirs.

"We'll pretend that we're not in a small space, then," he said. "Would you mind if I suggested… that is, why don't you close your eyes for a bit?"

He laughed as her eyes opened wider. "That isn't exactly what I meant, sunshine."

"I know. I just…" She took a deep shuddery breath.

"It's just so you won't see where you are, then you won't think about it so much. I won't touch you," he said. "I promise. Here, put your hand on the phone. If I do anything or say anything you don't like, even slightly, you call for help. I don't think they'll have any difficulty identifying me as the culprit once they get us out of here."

She almost managed a smile. He was glad that by keeping her talking, she was forgetting her fears for a moment. "Close your eyes," he whispered. And her lashes drifted shut, hiding those gorgeous hazel eyes from his view.

"What now?" she asked.

"How about this? Picture something wonderful," he suggested. "Someplace really big and open. The ocean."

She laughed softly, a low husky sound that would have been right at home in a setting that included satin sheets, candles and a man's fingertips caressing her skin. "I've never been to the ocean."

"Hmm, well, you should go someday," he said, even though he'd never been to the ocean, either. "You should definitely insist that your husband take you there." It didn't hurt to remind himself that she probably was some man's treasure, and he, Ace Turner Carson, had no business thinking of her in connection with satin sheets, candles or touching.

Her eyes flew open, and he didn't have to ask why. "No husband," he deduced automatically. "Well, all right, then. No husband, but you look like a very independent woman. You obviously are a busy and capable woman. You still have that clipboard," he teased. "And you've made it clear that you don't need any help from a man. You can transport yourself to the ocean. You *are* a career woman, aren't you?" he asked, indicating the pin she wore that said Mission Creek Memorial staff. "You probably hate the fact that one of the first things men notice about you is your legs."

Her cheeks turned a delicious shade of rose. Embarrassment or anger? he wondered. Actually he hoped he hadn't embarrassed her when what he'd been aiming for was a little indignation on her part. Anger was a good thing at times. It could take a person's mind off his or her problems. He knew about using anger to run from troubles.

"My legs?" she asked as if she hadn't heard him right. Maybe she hadn't when she was so frightened she could barely think, much less hear.

"Absolutely beautiful," he said, wondering what in hell he was doing and where this was leading.

But just at that moment the elevator began to move again. The beauty gasped. Reality sank in. She smiled in relief, automatically turning to him to share the moment.

He smiled back, entranced by the sheer joy on her face.

And then the elevator stopped again.

Ace didn't give her time even to think about the fact that salvation had been stolen from her. He didn't want to see what that kind of fear and disappointment could do to her. Instead, he swooped in close, crowding her, knowing that the nearness of his body would be a distraction, although probably an unwelcome one for a woman such as this. ''Tell me what that pin is for and why you were carrying that clipboard,'' he said, searching for a topic to take her mind off her troubles.

The clipboard was still on the floor at her feet. To see it, she'd have to look down. Her hair would no doubt brush against him, he was that close. Instead, she looked up into his eyes, her own uncertain and slightly lost. She fingered the pin on her lapel. ''I'm...that is, I'm the hospital fund-raiser.'' She swallowed hard and then squared her shoulders. ''You probably already know, but today is a very big day for the hospital with the new ward opening and so many people coming for the celebration. Lots to think about and keep track of. Lots to do,'' she said, her voice a soft whisper. After all, he was near. Near enough to breathe in the floral scent of her shampoo. There was no need to raise her voice.

For a minute with this soft lovely woman standing beside him, Ace wasn't sure he'd be able to speak as the threads of desire wound through his body. But though he had her talking, he was reasonably certain that he needed to *keep* her talking. Otherwise, she was going to remember where they were. The fear would resurface with a vengeance.

''You're the hospital's fund-raiser? Ah, so you are an independent woman, darlin'.''

She lifted her chin, tipping her head back and causing her hair to spill over her shoulders. Some of her former color and life seemed to have returned. ''You're trying to get a rise out of me, aren't you. So that I won't think about the fact that I want to physically rip the doors off their tracks with my teeth."

Okay, so she was on to him. "That would be fun to watch," he conceded.

"It's not going to work, you know," she said. "This isn't the first time someone has tried to talk me out of this irrational behavior. I can't seem to control it, hard as I try. You might as well give up. But I do appreciate your efforts…"

"Ace," he said automatically, though she hadn't asked his name. Oh, yes, he knew about irrational behavior, because for some reason he wanted to hear his name on her lips.

"Ace," she repeated, her voice as soft as a whisper in the dark of night. The small space they occupied could well have been a bed. He was close enough to reach out and pull her to him, to taste her lips. He was staring down into her eyes. Her breathing was coming quickly.

But of course her breathing was coming quickly. She was scared to death.

Ace backed away a few inches. "So now you know *my* name, darlin'," he offered.

She let out a laugh. "I get your point, and you're right. I've already told you my occupation, one of my deepest fears and revealed the fact that I'm not married. It's silly to keep my name from you, when I assume you're here for the ribbon-cutting ceremony and I'll be in front of the crowd." She looked toward the darn buttons.

"Soon," he said. "You'll be in front of the crowd soon. Would you like me to call again?"

He could tell that she wanted to say no, that she wanted to appear strong. "Yes, please," she said in a very small voice.

"Any word on our condition?" Ace asked the security guard on the other end. "Ten minutes?" It wasn't long, but the lady was clearly hoping for something more like ten seconds.

"I'm okay with that," she assured him rather unconvincingly. "And my name is Crystal. Crystal Bennett." Her words came out in a rush.

Ordinarily he would have offered his last name, too, but today wasn't a day for the ordinary ways. And revealing his last name to Crystal Bennett would fill her with questions that would probably take her mind off their situation, but would simply complicate other things. The Carsons had supplied a fair share of the money for the new wing. He'd heard that from every gas-station attendant and convenience-store clerk he'd spoken to in the course of getting directions around the city. The largest donors to the new wing and the hospital's chief fund-raiser would, out of necessity, have a good relationship. Revealing his identity to Crystal would only lead to questions about his intent, and that just wasn't a good idea right now.

"Crystal's an exceptionally pretty name," he said, instead, meaning it.

Another blush kissed her cheeks. Ace couldn't remember ever spending time with a woman who actually blushed. The women he consorted with were completely foreign to the concept of innocence, and pretty much nothing embarrassed them. He ought to view this as a sign. A huge red stop sign.

"How long have we been in here, do you think?" she asked.

A few minutes, but he knew what she meant. It seemed longer, and it was beginning to seem longer still when Ace looked down at the shining crown of her hair and breathed in deeply. The floral scent of her hair mingled with something that smelled suspiciously like soap. Whatever it was, it was sexy as hell, and suddenly he was very aware that she was all soft skin and big trusting eyes. Oh, yes, that was trust he was seeing there.

"We'll be out soon," he said again, fighting to keep the husky note from his voice.

She nodded and bit her lip. "I wish I'd borrowed someone's cell phone. I promised my son I would come and see him before the ceremonies began. He's in the day-care center. He's too young to tell time, but once things get started, he'll hear the music and know that things are starting."

"You have a son." Ace forced the words through his lips. She had a son. And no husband. This probably wasn't something he wanted to know.

For the first time he surprised a genuine no-holds-barred smile from her lips. "Timmy," she said, and it was clear from that one word that her entire world circled around her little boy. "He's just three."

"Does he look like you?" Ace asked. Anything to keep that light in her eyes.

"No, like his father." She dug into her purse and found a picture. She handed it to Ace. There, smiling back at him, was the cutest little dark-haired, big-eyed munchkin he'd ever seen.

"You're wrong," he said. "He has your eyes."

"Well, maybe," she conceded, "but nothing else."

"You'll give him other things," Ace said with the confidence of a man who knew what he was talking about. "Does his father live nearby?" Why had he asked that question?

A question he obviously shouldn't have asked, since the smile on Crystal's lips died. "Timmy's father never wanted to be a part of his life. He took off as soon as he knew the baby was on the way."

A knifelike and familiar pain sliced through Ace.

"His loss," he said tensely.

"Exactly," she said with great feeling. And their eyes met. They shared a commiserating look. For long seconds Ace's gaze held her gaze. He studied her. She had the most beautiful expressive mouth, he couldn't help thinking. A mouth made for deep slow kisses that went on and on and led to better things. He could almost see how Timmy's father had lost his head and ended up fathering a child because he, too, had a strong urge to step close to Crystal and pull her into his arms. And with a woman like this, that kind of thing could only lead to other things.

Most likely me getting my face slapped, he thought with a smile.

"Ace?" Crystal asked, and he realized that she was probably wondering why he was grinning.

"You probably don't want to know, but I was thinking about how tasty your lips look," he said, and he heard her sharp intake of air. Well, hell, he *had* always been known for speaking his mind. No doubt, this would have been one time when he should have stifled his speech and his thoughts.

"But I meant what I said before, Crystal. I don't force myself on women. You're safe with me."

She studied him for a minute. Suddenly the elevator began moving again, and it continued to move until it reached the main floor and the doors opened.

Ace held out his hand, motioning for Crystal to exit the elevator in front of him. She turned to go, then turned back. Her small hand touched his sleeve, and she looked up at him.

"You made me feel safe," she said. "I know you were trying to distract me to keep my mind off things. You're a kind man, Ace. Thank you."

He simply stared down at her, then watched as she walked away. She might think he was a kind man now, but what was she going to think later today when he publicly embarrassed one of the hospital's biggest benefactors?

Crystal moved out into the sunshine where tables and booths and a podium for speeches had been set up. A wide blue-and-white ribbon cordoned off the new and shiny maternity wing, which had taken so much time and effort from so many. She had spent the past two years of her life working toward this day, yet now that it was here, all she could think about was the man she'd met in the elevator.

A small smile lifted her lips. He'd certainly been handsome with that wavy black hair and those blue eyes. And that smile. Her heart flipped at the memory.

"Stop it," she told herself. "You know darn well

that a man like that has used that smile on a million women. He's slid into a hundred women's beds just because they couldn't resist that devilish grin and all that sweet talking.''

She'd been barely able to resist, either, but *barely* was the operative word here, because she was darn well going to resist even thinking about the man. If there was one woman in all of Mission Creek who knew better than to fall for a pair of let's-make-love-darlin' blue eyes and a rogue's smile, it was her.

No more handsome heartbreakers for her, now or ever. She had Timmy to think of. And that was all the reminder Crystal needed.

Besides, today was a workday. People were relying on her. And there was a ton of things that still had to be taken care of, a fact that became clear as she neared the area where the ribbon-cutting ceremony was due to begin shortly and her employees flocked around her with tales of minor crises and questions that needed to be answered.

Crystal took a deep breath and plunged in. Her last thought of Ace was that he would make a great lover, but a very bad husband. Not that it mattered. She wasn't even slightly interested in a husband.

And she was certainly going to keep her distance from Ace if he should show up at the ceremony.

TWO

Real impressive, Ace thought as he surveyed the lawns that surrounded the new maternity wing of the hospital. Lots of white damask tablecloths, polished silver, yellow and blue blossoms and champagne. Pretty expensive, very classy. A bit more formal than he was expecting. The Carson money that was supporting this fandango was clearly evident. Of course, his little redheaded fund-raiser was probably also responsible for procuring a great portion of that donation. He could just picture her opening those big hazel eyes wide. In two seconds flat all those rich lecherous Carson men would have been fighting each other and everyone else to be the first to pull out their wallets. Not that she would use flirtation to get her way. That was clearly not her style at all, Ace reminded himself. That didn't mean that his half brothers wouldn't want her, though. Any man would.

He'd been wandering around the room while the speeches went on, observing the crowd. Now he wondered how well his half brothers knew Crystal, if they were the type who could charm women into their beds, and if they'd view a woman alone like Crystal as fair game. He'd heard that his siblings were married, but then, there were plenty of men who didn't view marriage as a deterrent to their pleasure, and plenty of wives who were willing to look the other way. No doubt all the Carson men were charming. His mother had told him that his father was.

And the rest of the Carsons had a few things Ace didn't have. Money. Success. Respectability.

Oh, no, he wasn't the least bit respectable and he never tried to be. If there was one prime rule he lived by it was Never pretend you're something you're not. Never be a wanna-be. He'd learned that lesson very well, had had it impressed upon him at an early age.

"So just get every thought of Crystal Bennett out of your mind," he told himself. "Time to go to work, Ace."

He moved across the springy grass toward the crowd. Out of the corner of his eye he saw Crystal, her head bent toward a young man who was gesticulating wildly with his hands and holding up what looked to be a spoon. Crystal gave the man a long soulful look, said a few words, and then the young man's face broke into a smile before he moved away.

"Looks like one crisis averted," Ace said with a chuckle. Now to his own situation. It appeared the presentations were over, and people were starting to mingle on the grounds and attack the food. It was time to begin meeting his new temporary neighbors.

"Good afternoon, ma'am," he said to a large sixtyish woman wearing a hot-pink dress and lots of clanking bracelets. "Nice party, isn't it? Allow me to introduce myself. I'm Ace Turner Carson. Lovely dress you're wearing. That color most definitely brings out the pretty roses in your cheeks." He tilted his head and smiled at her.

She giggled. "Thank you, sir, and yes, it *is* a nice party. Ace Turner *Carson*, did you say? Not one of *our* Carsons?"

Ah, she'd asked the right question.

"I hope you'll consider me yours," he said with a wink.

The woman giggled again and almost fluttered her eyelashes, wishing him well as he moved on through the crowd. Glancing around the room, Ace looked over people's heads and located Crystal. She was looking his way, but when his gaze caught hers, she quickly glanced away.

Just as well. He didn't know why he was so aware of her presence, anyway. It wasn't right. He hadn't come to town to connect with anyone, and when he was done here, he planned to move on. Quickly. No looking back. So it was best if he stopped looking around for the lady right now. She had those vulnerable eyes, and he was a man who would only hurt her, especially considering his feelings about dating women with children. Children needed contact with responsible adults. Responsibility wasn't exactly one of his strong suits, either. Best to remember that, he thought with a frown.

Wandering near a group of men debating the merits of opening the new maternity wing, he started to pass them by, then thought better of it.

"The old hospital was what we had for years and it was just fine," one man said. "All this money spent for nothing."

Ace cast him an amused look, which caught the man's attention.

"What does that look mean?" the man asked, bristling.

"Not a thing," Ace said, holding out his hands in a gesture of innocence. "Just that I was thinking that having a new maternity wing probably means room for lots more babies, and there's only one way I know to get more babies. Can't imagine why a man would be complaining about that."

The rest of the men in the group chuckled, and finally the bristling one shrugged sheepishly and laughed along with them. "Bet you've had your share of women wanting to make babies, too," he shot back. "You new around here?"

"I sure am. Name's Ace. Ace Turner Carson. No babies to my name, but I do like all the activities that lead up to them," he said, slapping the man on the back and moving away before anyone could ask him about his name.

That was the point for now. To get just a few people buzzing and wondering. Could he be related to the mighty and well-respected Ford Carson?

"Oh, yeah," Ace whispered to himself. The great Ford Carson wasn't quite as respectable as everyone thought. After all, he'd fathered an illegitimate son and then left the son's mother to fend for herself. Not such an exemplary character, after all, was he? And neither was the son. In fact, he could be quite a thorn in a person's side, if he wanted to be.

He definitely wanted to be.

The buzz behind him grew a bit. He heard the name

Carson mentioned once or twice. He moved on, staying to himself for the most part, but now and then stopping to plant a seed.

"Not too fast, Ace," he told himself. "We want to stretch this out. Let it bloom and grow over weeks. Let the doubt and the questions begin to build slowly."

He saw several men glance his way. They looked a lot like the pictures he'd seen of his half brothers, but he wasn't ready to meet them yet, and he knew how to evade someone when he wanted to. He moved on.

And then he looked up and saw Crystal again, her pretty hair slipping over her shoulders. He practically willed her to look up at him, and she did. He could almost hear her sharp intake of air. He could almost see the delicate blush that covered her cheekbones and no doubt all of her honey-and-cream skin as well.

For half a second he held her gaze, but she quickly turned away.

Ace felt a slight twinge of anger at himself. He wanted her to look at him. Longer. More meaningfully. With desire in her eyes and on her lips. Actually, he wanted her to come closer. Close enough to touch.

She was a vision in pale blue, surrounded by men in suits, all looking at her as if they'd offer her the world if she'd just smile at one of them.

But then, some men didn't have the world to offer. They just drifted from one thing to the next, rootless, and liked it that way. Liked it very much.

Ace forced himself to look away from Crystal.

"Ace Carson," he said to a man he met a few minutes later. A doctor from the hospital by the looks of things. "Nice town you have here. Nice hospital, too."

"Glad you like the place. We do, too. My name's Jared Cross," he said, holding out his hand. "I work here. Child psychiatry. Family planning."

"Family planning? Then you're involved in this new wing?"

"I have a definite interest, yes," the man said. "We have a well-known fertility clinic here. It all ties together. I'm really pleased Mission Creek Memorial pulled this off. It was quite a feat. Lots of work and dedication."

The man's comments confirmed what Ace had begun to suspect. For such a little thing, Crystal had a big impact on people. She took her work seriously. Again Ace scanned the room for her. Finally he located her, holding court in the middle of a crowd of obviously wealthy benefactors. He relaxed and turned back to find Jared grinning.

"She's something, isn't she?" Jared said.

"I wouldn't really know. I just arrived in town. But yes, she is intriguing," he said, unwilling to let on just how intriguing he found her. And how unnerving it was to find himself lusting after a woman he had no business lusting after. It was obvious she was not only a serious innocent, but he was beginning to learn that she had major ties to the Carsons through this hospital and also through Fiona Carson Martin, his little half sister who was also involved in fund-raising. He'd heard it whispered that they were friends.

"So the woman's intriguing?" Jared repeated with a knowing grin. "In my opinion, the woman is a wonder. She's fervent about the need for this wing, and it shows in everything she's said and done to make this project work. She probably had people fighting to be the first to get in the door with their money."

The obvious admiration in his voice didn't escape Ace's notice. Neither did the fact that most women would find Cross's black hair and green eyes irresistible. A powerful surge of something possessive streaked through Ace, and he frowned slightly.

"You have an interest in the lady?" Ace couldn't stop himself from asking, even though he cursed himself for doing so.

Jared raised one brow. "Of course. A purely professional one." He frowned. "What did you say your last name was? Carson? Does that mean you're related to the Mission Creek Carsons?"

Ace shrugged. "I never knew my father. Do I look like a Mission Creek Carson to you?" He chuckled, flipping open his jacket to reveal the frayed dark blue lining.

"I get your point," Jared said. "The Carsons own a substantial chunk of the town."

"I guess I don't qualify, then. Pleased to have met you, though." He shook Jared's hand and began to move on, his gaze sweeping the room.

"She's over there," Jared said with a grin, indicating Crystal's new location.

Ace chuckled. "Okay, I'm more than intrigued," he admitted as he nodded to Cross and moved away.

He also admitted that he had probably done enough

for tonight. The framework of what he intended was in place. He ought to be pleased. People were wondering who he was. They were finding out that he was a bit of a flirt, a bit of a tease, illegitimate, possibly a fly-by-night but amiable rogue, and they were beginning to wonder if he couldn't, in some way, be related to Ford Carson.

Ace glanced around at the men he'd identified earlier as Carsons from the descriptions he'd been given. Matt, Flynt. Ford didn't appear to be here. At least not yet.

No matter. He had time and patience.

He scanned the room, looking to see if his target was arriving, but at that moment he saw Crystal again. She was standing in a corner, nearly against a wall, and a thin man with dirty-blond hair and a goatee was watching her from across the lawn. Somehow, unlike the other men who had surrounded her earlier, this one didn't look as if he was waiting for her to smile. He didn't look as if he'd even noticed that the lady had soft pink lips made for kissing again and again. He looked extremely upset.

Moreover, he looked as if he had business with Crystal. Not good business, either, Ace surmised, as the man began to take quick, deliberate steps toward her.

Just then, a woman came up to Ace and started talking to him. Ace listened with only one ear.

But while he listened he had a feeling that, wise or not, he was going to end up speaking to Crystal Bennett again.

Soon.

He only hoped he would remember she was a lady,

a vulnerable lady, and he was a man she wasn't going to like for very long. Not if she liked this town and the true Carsons.

Crystal could feel Ace's eyes on her. Every time she'd looked up, it seemed, he had been grinning, flirting with the women gathered here, who were all beginning to fan themselves whenever he drew near.

Not that she could blame them. He was tall enough to make a woman feel faint, his blue eyes promised long nights of raw pleasure, and his mouth...well, just thinking about that slash of a mouth made her stomach flutter.

She'd had to keep reminding herself that she was here to ensure a smooth party and a flawless ceremony. Besides, she didn't go near good-looking flirts anymore. She'd had more than her share of them in so many ways. But oh, my, Ace was going to fuel some very powerful fantasies tonight. Not just hers, either. She bet that half the women in the room were going to dream of him in their beds tonight, dropping feverish kisses on their naked skin.

She fanned herself with a program.

"Well, look here what I've found. If it isn't little Crystal Bennett still looking like the slut she is."

Crystal gave a start at the familiar, raspy voice from her past. To her chagrin, her first move on hearing the ugly accusation was to look down at her suit. Although her outfit ended just above her knee, it was very demure, a plain skirt and short-sleeved jacket that were neither too snug nor cut too low.

She forced herself to look up, despite the fear spiraling through her, nearly choking her. Branson Hines stood before her, his lank dirty hair disheveled, his black eyes slightly crazed. He was staring at her jacket as if he could see right through it.

Automatically, she raised her hand to cover herself. She reminded herself that she was in a crowded gathering, even if she was standing in a rather deserted area at the moment, beneath the shadow of some trees. Besides, she was a grown woman now. She didn't have to let Branson intimidate her anymore.

"Branson," she said as smoothly as she could manage, pretending he had said nothing out of the ordinary. "I hope you're enjoying the ceremonies." She didn't hold out her hand as she would have to anyone else. "But I'm afraid I have business to attend to now. If you'll excuse me."

She tried to move around him to head back to the relative safety of the more crowded area.

He put one hand across her path. She changed direction and he grabbed her wrist.

"You don't like being called a slut, Crystal? I don't see why not," he said. "After all, that's what you are, isn't it? Your son is a bastard, isn't he? You let his father into your bed when you weren't married. How many men have there been since then? Or do you just say yes to every man who wants you?"

Panic and fear rose in her throat. His grip on her wrist tightened as he leaned close enough for her to smell his sour breath. His grimy fingers cut into her skin.

"Let me go, Branson," she said, trying to sound

calm. She would not make a scene or allow him to ruin the proceedings for the maternity wing. Branson was not a huge man. Surely she could get away. Years ago there had been another day when he had made ugly remarks to her, but he had never actually tried to hurt her. At least not physically.

"Oh, I don't think I'll let you go just yet," he said, reeling her in. "You share your favors with other men you're not married to, but I've never even touched you. I always wanted to touch you."

She opened her mouth. To order him away or to scream, she wasn't sure which.

But he yanked her hard and pulled her up against him. A cry ripped from her throat as she shoved at him and tried to keep his lips from getting near hers. Her wrists were burning as he twisted them and held fast, shoving his face into hers.

"Please. No," she said. "Don't."

"I never even had a kiss," he said. He pressed his wet lips to hers. She fought the blackness that threatened to envelop her as he tried to hold her still and she struggled to pull away. His laughter mocked her pitiful efforts.

And then she was free, the cool air rushing over her face. Branson was kicking at someone. She blinked to clear her eyes and saw that Ace had Branson's arm pulled up behind his back.

"You don't want to touch a lady who hasn't invited you," Ace said, his voice low and cold. "That's not exactly the way to win points with a woman. It's definitely not a gentlemanly thing to do, now is it?"

Branson swore and tried to wrest his arm free. "She's not exactly a lady in my book."

Ace spun Branson around, shoving him up against a tree, his arm lodged against Branson's windpipe, leaving him barely enough air to breathe, judging by Branson's choked gurgling. "Then maybe you've been reading the wrong book, buddy. Now, I'm going to ease up on you real slow, and I want you to tell the lady you're sorry you touched her, that you're sorry you even dared to come near her."

Ace eased the pressure on Branson's throat, and the man muttered an even fouler word. He tried to break free.

With barely a shrug, Ace slammed Branson up against the tree again, hard enough to send a few leaves fluttering to the ground. "Let's try this again, shall we, buddy?" he said, leaning in to apply more pressure. "You want to reconsider that apology?"

Crystal didn't want an apology from Branson. She just wanted him gone. But there was such steel in Ace's voice and he was so focused on what he was doing that she didn't want to distract him for fear Branson would pull free and strike out, catching Ace off guard.

"I'm really starting to lose patience with your lack of good manners. You ready with that apology yet, pal?" Ace asked.

Branson raised dark, hate-filled eyes to Crystal. "Sorry," he said, the word clipped and barely audible.

She gave him a curt nod just as a security guard approached. "Thanks, man. We'll take him off your hands," he told Ace. "Ms. Fiona saw that something was happening and sent us over, Ms. Bennett. We'll get him out of here right away," he promised.

"Thank you," she breathed.

But her words were nearly drowned out by Branson's sudden shouting as the security guard removed a pair of handcuffs from his belt.

"You tramp, Crystal, you're gonna pay for this. I know how you operate. I know who and what you are. You're a backstabber. You promise things and then don't deliver. But I know that, and I'll be back. I'll be lookin' for you. You and your kind took something I wanted. Now maybe I'll take something *you* want, and I do know what means the most to you. Don't think I don't."

His words were spewed out, dark and ominous. He lunged furiously, nearly dragging to the ground the security guard, who had only Branson's right wrist cuffed. Finally another security guard grabbed Branson's other arm, and together they cuffed his hands behind his back and pulled him from the area.

The silence that followed was like a thick choking smoke. Crystal's heart was beating frantically. What had he meant? What was he going to do?

She surprised herself by raising her gaze to Ace as if just looking at him could calm her. He was standing nearer than she'd expected. When her eyes met his, he moved closer and wrapped an arm around her waist.

"Go ahead. Lean on me," he whispered, then looked up at the small crowd who'd gathered.

"I tell you, some people just shouldn't even go to

parties," he said, addressing the group. "That one there looks like he started drinking early and needs to sleep it off. I guess he just didn't like it when Ms. Bennett suggested he leave and get some rest. But it *was* a pretty good demonstration of the security at Mission Creek Memorial, though, wasn't it? You can all rest easy knowing you'll always be safe here. Makes you feel good seeing this hospital is on the job protecting the people staying here, doesn't it?" He smiled reassuringly on that last note, and everyone began to murmur among themselves and drift away. One or two of them gave Crystal a worried look, but somehow she managed to follow Ace's lead and paste on a smile. In spite of the fact that her heart was still hammering.

Slowly, almost without her noticing it, Ace walked her into the deeper shelter of some trees where some small benches were positioned. He eased her down on one, and she realized that her legs had been a bit shaky and she'd been leaning on Ace, an almost total stranger.

She glanced up at him, wondering what he really thought about what had happened back there. Especially since she herself wasn't quite sure what had happened. She hadn't seen Branson in years.

But Ace's expression was unreadable. He bore no sign of his struggle with Branson other than one disheveled lock of black hair. He looked like a man who was used to fighting and didn't let it bother him. It bothered her that he had been forced to come to her rescue.

"I seem to be causing you a great deal of trouble today," she said.

He ignored her concerned tone and gave her a slow sexy grin. "Don't apologize. I'm rather partial to trouble. Been in the thick of it all my life."

She gulped at the look in his eyes. It was the look a man gives a woman who interests him, at least physically. Her pulse began to trip over itself. This just wouldn't do. It wasn't that she didn't find him amazingly attractive. She did, and more than that, she was grateful for his help and his kind attention, more grateful than she could say. But he was obviously the worst kind of man. The kind that flipped through women like the pages of a magazine. The kind she never went near, not anymore.

"Well, then, all I can say is thank you for your help. I'm indebted to you," she said. "If I can ever repay you..." She hoped that didn't sound as bad to him as it did to her.

He shook his head. "For what? I told you, I welcome trouble."

Oh, she'd just bet he did. She'd bet he caused it, too. Which meant the only smart thing for her to do now was to get as far away as possible from the attraction he held for her. "Thank you, anyway," she said. "But I guess I should get back and make sure everything is running smoothly."

He nodded, but the long look he gave her held her as immobile as Branson's death grip. "You want to tell me what that was all about back there?"

Three

Crystal blinked. No, she didn't want to talk about what had happened with Branson. She didn't want to talk about it or even think about it. But Ace stood there waiting, his blue eyes studying her, his stance loose, almost relaxed.

As if he could wait forever for her to speak.

"I don't exactly know," she finally confessed. "Years ago, when I was in high school, I dated Branson. He seemed like a quiet shy boy at first. After we'd gone out once or twice, though, he...well, I could tell that he wasn't always operating under the same rules as the rest of the world. Little things upset him a lot more than they did most people. He would get unreasonably angry if he forgot his textbook at home, angry enough to throw things. If I didn't say 'Goodbye, Branson,' instead of just 'Goodbye,' he would rant and rave. After just two dates I told him that I didn't think I was right for him and that he should find someone else."

She stared into Ace's eyes. She was embarrassed, and her first instinct was to look down, but she'd done enough of that in her life and so she forced herself to hold his gaze.

Instead, he was the one to glance down. Just once.

Just a quick look. She realized she was twisting her hands together. So much for appearing poised and calm.

"I take it Branson wasn't exactly happy with your decision."

She wasn't sure she could say the next part. She wasn't sure why she was even considering saying anything, but there was something very compelling about Ace's unreadable expression. It was the sort of expression a cop might wear. *Just the facts, ma'am,* he seemed to be saying. And she realized she'd never really told anyone about what had happened between her and Branson. Maybe because all of them thought they already knew and no one wanted to talk about it.

"Branson blew up. He screamed and yelled. In the end he begged. I was...I was frightened, but I knew that it would be worse giving in than going forward. I left. Soon after that, the whispers started. Someone started a rumor that I was easy, that I would let anyone do anything, that I would sleep with any male who asked, that I was a tramp. Branson told them that I'd done things with him that I'd never done. Most people didn't believe him, but a few did. That hurt so much that I went into hiding, which was the wrong thing to do. People took it as an admission of guilt. It took me years to win back my self-esteem. And then I met John. I had Timmy out of wedlock. The rumors started again, only this time I stared them down. The Carsons found me a good job here at the hospital, and I hold my head up high."

"No reason you shouldn't," Ace said softly.

She realized that she'd made her last statement somewhat defensively, but that Ace hadn't seemed to notice.

"Anyway, that's my story, such as it is. I haven't had contact with Branson for years. He's spent a lot of time in and out of jail. He did have some conflict with the hospital once in the not-too-distant past. His wife had experienced complications of childbirth due to alcohol abuse, and the doctors were unable to save the baby, which was premature. Branson tried to sue, unsuccessfully. For the past year, he's been in jail for burglarizing an auto parts store, so I have no idea what brought him here today or why he chose to approach me. What I do know is that I really had better get back to work now."

Ace gazed down at her. She stood up and he stepped aside to let her past.

"Thank you for stepping in to help me," she said, holding out her hand.

He stared down at her hand, and for a moment her palm tingled. Then he closed his fingers around hers. His hand was large and warm, but she didn't feel threatened the way she had with Branson. Instead, she felt a desire to stay there connected to him. Quickly she withdrew her hand and turned away.

He fell into step beside her.

She glanced to the side and frowned. "I know I've twice looked like a helpless boob today, but I assure you that I can take care of myself."

"I know that." He continued walking by her side.

"I really don't think he's going to come back and bother me again."

"Probably not."

"The security officers took him away. He's gone."

"Looks that way."

"Ace, you don't need to escort me. I'm not going to get in any more trouble."

He raised one lazy brow and she held back a smile. She couldn't really blame him, considering the way the day had gone.

"I'm not normally this catastrophe-prone," she promised, and this time she wasn't sure whether she was talking to him or to herself.

He stopped, turning to face her, and took both her hands in his. "Everyone knows that. I can't tell you how many total strangers have told me that you are the one responsible for this new wing. I believe the way they put it was 'Crystal Bennett can turn on that smile and talk you into donating money you haven't even started to earn yet.'"

She laughed. "Well, I'm not that bad—or that good—but we really did need this maternity wing."

"The hospital didn't handle births?"

"Of course they did, but everything was old, kind of cold and sterile. It's very…well, it's frightening when you have your first baby. Lots of the mothers are young. They're scared. They need to know that their babies are going to get the best care and that they're going to be born into a warm welcoming world. This new wing is designed to make having a baby much safer and less distressing."

Ace gazed down at her with fierce blue eyes. "Is that how it was for you? Frightening?"

Oh, no. She hadn't meant to bring out those protective instincts in him again. Even though she *had* been frightened giving birth to Timmy alone.

"I was a lioness," she managed to say with a straight face.

He chuckled and brushed a finger across her cheek. "I'll bet you were," he said. "Now come on."

"Where are we going?"

"I've been watching you all afternoon. It's getting late, and you've been so busy that you haven't eaten."

"I'll eat," she promised, "but I'm still working. When it's over, I'll definitely be fed," she said, lifting her chin as he gave her one of those I-don't-believe-you looks. "Don't worry about me. Like I told you, I know how to take care of myself. I'm used to it and I like it," she said firmly.

"Oh, but it's not nearly as much fun as having a gorgeous man take over for a while, Crystal." A soft teasing voice sounded at Crystal's shoulder and she turned to see Fiona Carson Martin smiling at her and Ace.

"Fiona," Crystal said with a smile. "I'm glad to see you could make it. Is everything all right?"

Fiona laughed. "Yes, very all right. I'm sorry I was late, but I was almost ready to slip my dress on when…well, my husband can be quite a distraction."

Crystal felt the warm color climbing her cheeks. She tried not to look at Ace, but couldn't seem to help herself. He was smiling at her.

"Speaking of distractions, Crystal, why don't you introduce me to your young man? He seems to be causing quite a stir. The family sent me over to find out his story. They all feel very protective toward you, you know."

Honestly, could a woman get any warmer or pinker? "Mr.—Ace is a new acquaintance," Crystal replied. "Fiona Carson Martin, meet Ace…" She looked up at him expectantly, waiting for him to fill in his last name.

For a moment there was silence. She thought she'd seen a muscle twitch in his jaw when she introduced Fiona, but that must have been her imagination. Nothing had fazed Ace today, not being trapped in an elevator or fighting off a violent lunatic. Why should he mind being introduced to a beautiful woman? For a second Crystal felt a pain in her heart. A ridiculous pain, she assured herself. Of course she didn't care how Ace reacted to Fiona or any other woman.

She looked up at Ace, who still hadn't spoken.

His frozen expression relaxed into a smile, almost as if he had willed it to please her. "Sorry, you caught me a bit off guard there," he said. "My name's Ace Carson, son of Ford Carson. Perhaps you know him?"

Suddenly Crystal couldn't breathe.

Fiona blinked and looked as if she couldn't think. But then, true to character, she managed to smile.

"Well, my goodness, isn't this an incredibly interesting turn? And yes, I might know Ford," she said. "You and Daddy talk often, do you?"

Her voice issued a challenge.

Ace gave her a long, slow and very cold grin. "Never met the man."

Fiona nodded. "I see."

"I don't think you do."

"You're probably right." She studied him for long seconds. "Just out of curiosity, how old are you?"

Crystal focused her attention on her friend, who looked as if her expression had frozen in place.

"Thirty-six," Ace finally said, clipping off the words.

A bit of life flowed back into Fiona's face and she shrugged. "Older than my oldest brother, Flynt. I guess that makes it all right. If it's true."

Ace didn't respond to that. Crystal could see, though, that it didn't make it all right with him. His eyes were hard, his jaw tense. Fiona could probably see that, too. She never missed much.

"Would you like to meet Daddy?" she asked softly.

For a minute Crystal thought Ace wasn't going to answer. Then he shrugged. "I'll meet him." Which wasn't quite the same as saying he'd *like* to meet him, Crystal couldn't help noting.

"Come on, I'll introduce you," Fiona offered. "He's not here today. He's been a little under the weather these past couple of days, and since he could only manage one party today, he chose to attend the one at the country club, his home away from home. It'll be starting in just a few minutes now that things are winding down here. Crystal, I know you were planning on attending. Do you want to come along with us?"

No, she didn't. Now more than ever, she knew that Ace was dangerous. Dangerous in ways she didn't understand. And he was really still a stranger, even more so now. A handsome, intriguing stranger who made her knees weak, who filled her with desire she didn't understand and didn't really want to acknowledge.

And now he appeared to be here for some reason known only to him. He was a man of mystery. Not even remotely safe.

Above all, she wanted a life filled with security and safety.

She didn't want to follow Ace Carson anywhere.

But he was obviously facing a few difficult moments, and she just didn't seem to be able to stop herself.

"Let's go see Ford," she said. And for some reason she couldn't understand, she reached out and took Ace's hand. She did her very best to ignore the foolish feeling that she wanted that hand sliding down her back someday, urging her close.

Because right now she had a feeling that Ace just needed a hand to hold, and that he wasn't used to feeling that way.

Tomorrow they were both going to regret this moment. But right now she had today to contend with.

She'd become very good at never looking at tomorrow, at the possibilities or disappointments the next day might bring. Now she had to work at it even harder.

Now there was Ace.

Temptation.

She wondered if she was strong enough to resist the pull of him. Above all, she didn't want to wake up alone in bed one day soon with the imprint of a man's body on her sheets and his license plate fading away in the distance. Not again. Never again.

But she wouldn't think about that now.

"Are you really Ford's son?" she whispered.

Blue eyes met hers. She shivered.

"Afraid so," he said. "And I'm real sorry about all this."

Crystal closed her eyes. The last time a man had said something like that to her, he had been leaving. And her life had never been the same.

"So are you really related to us?" Fiona asked Ace a few minutes later.

He nodded and looked down into Fiona's inquisitive green eyes. "You don't look very surprised," he said.

She laughed. "You don't look like any Carson I've ever met before. Besides, surprised or not, I'm good at hiding things when I have to. And maybe I just don't believe you."

"Fiona," Crystal said, and he swung his gaze to the woman who had grasped his hand as if trying to protect him, the lady who had been the focus of his attention all afternoon, despite his every effort to ignore her. Her hazel eyes were clouded with worry, and her grip on his hand was tight and cold. He gave himself a mental kick for letting her get caught in the middle of this charade between him and a family who, until now, hadn't known he even existed. He knew so little about her.

Only that some man—no, make that *two* men—had treated her badly.

His grip on her hand tightened, and she gave a soft gasp.

Immediately he released her. "I'm sorry," he said, "and don't go worrying about me. I'm not upset because Fiona thinks I may be lying." He wouldn't tell her that it was she he worried about. She'd already assured him several times today that she was fully able to manage her affairs. He wanted to smile at the memory of how hard she'd argued her case, but he refrained from doing so. He knew she was capable. Everyone had told him so, but if she thought there was a man in the world who wouldn't want to champion her whether she welcomed it or not, then she didn't know much about men. And she had been threatened tonight. He couldn't forget that. He didn't think she could either, even though she was doing an admirable job of trying. He supposed a woman alone did a lot of that. No, he *knew* a woman alone did a lot of that.

Plus, he had a feeling that, mother or not, Crystal Bennett did *not* know very much at all about men. She brought out a protective side of him—the urge to keep her close enough to watch over her—that he didn't like admitting to. It just didn't fit into his plans, plans he'd been making for three months. Maybe plans that had been born thirty-six years ago. Not the kind of thing he could let go of just because he was worried about one small, brave, fierce woman.

"So should I believe that you're really related to me, that my father sired you?" Fiona asked him, breaking into his thoughts. "And if I should, why should I?"

He shook his head. "I wouldn't if I were you. After all, you seem like a smart lady. You probably already know the rules. Never believe anything a man tells you."

She studied him for a second, then exchanged a disbelieving look with Crystal. "Even my husband?"

He smiled at her patient tone. "You're right, ma'am. I stand corrected. Never trust a man, unless he's proved himself by putting a ring on your finger."

"So once a man puts a ring on your finger, he becomes instantly trustworthy?" Crystal asked, crossing her arms and staring at him incredulously.

Ace blinked. He almost smiled at her combative stance. "Why do I feel like I'm caught in the sights of a rifle with the two of you firing the questions? But yes, I get your point, and you're absolutely right. Some men never do become trustworthy, ring or no ring." Like him, he supposed. Wasn't he here to disrupt the lives of people she no doubt cared about?

"Hmm, I'm offering to take you to meet my family, and you're telling me that you can't be trusted?" Fiona raised a brow.

"That's right," he said softly.

To his surprise, she suddenly smiled. "I think I like you, Ace. You're direct, no pretense. That's a Carson trait, you know."

Ace nearly groaned. He didn't want to have any Carson traits. The less he had in common with his so-called relatives the better.

Crystal seemed to sense his consternation. "Are you all right?" She gazed up at him with her pretty, worried eyes. For a moment he couldn't look away.

Fiona chuckled.

Immediately Ace and Crystal turned to her. "Something funny, little sister?" Ace asked.

"Just enjoying myself," she said. "You know, I had expected this event to be rather dull, in spite of all Crystal's hard work. How nice to find out I was wrong. Lots of surprises today." She looked pointedly at her friend, and Ace didn't miss Crystal's blush.

"Shall we go?" he asked. "No time like the present to meet up with the past."

His voice was nearly expressionless, and Fiona winced. "Maybe I'd better go ahead. Daddy's heart might need some warning of what he has in store. Can you make sure that Ace gets there in one piece, Crystal?"

Crystal laughed. "If you knew how my day had been going, you wouldn't be asking that. Still, I think Ace will probably manage to get us all there intact."

"All?" he asked.

"I'm sorry, I should have said something. I need to pick up my son. Will that be a problem? If it is, I know any number of other people who are going to the Lone Star. I'm sure it would be no problem to find someone to escort you there."

He gazed down at her totally trusting expression and felt something he didn't want to feel. Guilt? The lady didn't know what he had in mind. She was good at talking people into doing things, as evidenced by this stunning addition to the hospital she'd managed to procure funding for. She would just as easily obtain passage for him to the country club. He'd warned her that his intentions couldn't be trusted, and yet she was planning to help him find a ride to the country club, anyway. She was prepared to take on more work in finding him a ride. Because she was afraid that he would object to sharing a car with her little boy? What kind of a man would run from a child?

But he knew the answer. Any number of men. The boy's father. His own father.

"I'd like to meet Timmy," he said, even though he knew this was dangerous territory. The woman was enticing. He needed to keep his distance, and he had absolutely no business at all bringing another innocent into his mess. Especially a child.

No question, he was going to have to be careful where Crystal was concerned.

Maybe he'd better start thinking about that seriously right now, instead of thinking that he'd like to fold her into his arms and take anything that she was willing to give.

Four

"Hey, partner, that's a pretty neat hat you've got there," Ace said.

Crystal took her eyes off the road for a minute and looked at Ace. He was turned halfway in his seat, studying her son who was strapped safely into the back seat. From the corner of her eye she could see Timmy fingering the cowboy hat he'd been wearing lately. The quick shy smile on his little face nearly split her heart in two. He had so few dealings with men that he was always eager for their attention.

He stuck his feet straight out as far as he could.

"Got new boots," she heard him say as she turned her attention back to the road.

"Yep. Nice shiny ones," Ace agreed. "Your mom pick 'em out?"

Crystal didn't hear anything, which probably meant that Timmy was shaking his head.

"No? You did that all by yourself, wildcat?" Ace's voice was properly weighted with admiration.

Timmy giggled at the nickname, and she could tell that he liked it. "Mr. Ford picked 'em. New boots for me and us all."

Silence slid into the car. Uh-oh, she hadn't thought Timmy would even remember where the boots came from. It was true, though. Ford Carson frequently liked to spring surprises on the kids at the day-care center. For half a second she wondered if it was because of some lingering guilt over a son he'd fathered thirty-six years ago. Immediately she felt her own guilt. She liked Ford, and she refused to question his motives.

"For all of you?" Ace finally said. "Your mom, too?"

"Mommy? No," Timmy said with a laugh. "Ony kids."

"Mmm, I see."

But Crystal knew that Ace didn't. "It's just the kind of thing Ford does now and then," she said. "He drops by and asks the teachers at the hospital day-care center if there's anything that any of the kids need. If one of them needs a hat, they all get hats."

But once again she wondered what it had been like for Ace. When he had needed a new hat or boots, who had provided them? She couldn't help looking over at him.

"Don't do that," he said. "I know what you're thinking. It's not why I'm here. I'm not three years old anymore. I'm not here for revenge for *me*."

He glanced back at Timmy and she was grateful that he had at least considered her son's presence, that he didn't want to scare a child.

Still, she hadn't missed the intonation in Ace's statement. He was obviously here for revenge for *someone*, judging by his words. And in spite of what he'd said, the fact remained that Ace did not look like a man who was looking forward to a reunion. If Ford truly was his father, then with or without the intent of revenge, things were not going to be easy tonight.

For anyone. When Ford Carson was upset, the whole Carson clan was upset. Fiona had seemed amused by Ace's presence, but then, Crystal knew what Fiona had been thinking. She'd been viewing him as a convenient new man in town—a match for Crystal. Fiona was always doing that kind of thing. Fiona had been purposely avoiding the obvious problems with her family. Maybe she just didn't want to think about them. Maybe she knew she couldn't stop what was going to happen and so had decided to simply get things over with.

Crystal hazarded a glance at Ace. His jaw was set. Tall and strong, he radiated masculinity and power even sitting down. He seemed to fill up the space of her small car. He was a man you couldn't miss in a crowd, a man no woman would want to miss...unless she was a woman who had a problem with men.

Like me, Crystal thought.

She wondered if Fiona wasn't making a mistake in inviting Ace to this gathering where Carsons would be so prevalent. No Carson was easily forgettable, and it looked as if Ace Carson fit the mold perfectly.

She doubted that this would be something anyone could simply get through quickly. Ace Carson was here to make a difference.

A shiver ran through her at the thought.

"You all right?" he asked in that low sexy voice.

She smiled.

"What?" he said.

"I was just thinking how that should have been my

question. Are you all right with this? With going to the Lone Star Country Club? The Carsons and the Wainwrights run it, you know.''

"I know."

"Are you...hoping to become a member of the family?" Immediately she regretted the words. "I'm sorry. I shouldn't have asked that. It's none of my business."

"Don't be sorry. You've got a right to ask. I invaded your celebration. It's obvious my only reason for being there was to check out the Carson clan. As for wanting to be accepted, that's the last thing I want. I have no interest in being a part of the family."

Then what? she wanted to ask, and her very interest in Ace troubled her. She shouldn't be here with him. But then she remembered how he'd soothed her on the elevator, how he'd protected her from Branson, how he'd noticed Timmy's hat and boots and drawn a smile from her reserved child.

"I can't tell you what I'm going to say to my father when I finally meet him, but...well, you probably shouldn't be here with me," he said.

"You're not going to... You wouldn't hurt anyone, would you?"

He chuckled. "My mother's ghost would rise up and smack me good if I did. That's not what this is about," he assured her. "I don't beat up aging men."

But that aging man had once been a very young man, a dashing young man who apparently had seduced Ace's mother.

Crystal glanced at Ace and wondered how many women had fallen under *his* spell.

"I won't hit anyone," he promised. "I never intended that. And I would not subject you or Timmy to that." He nodded toward her little boy who had gotten bored with the grown-up talk and fallen asleep in his car seat, his cowboy hat slipping off his head to lie half-crushed beneath his chubby pink cheek.

She parked the car outside the massive structure of the country club in the large lot west of the main building, climbed from the car and circled round to free Timmy from his car seat. His body was heavy with sleep, his arms and legs rubbery, his head flopping over.

"I'll carry him," Ace said, and he took her son from her.

He held him reverently, her fatherless child. But Crystal also noticed that Ace stiffened slightly whenever the boy moved. And when she led him past the gardens, across the enormous porch, into the building and back to the nursery, he looked relieved to be divested of his package. It was obvious that though he seemed to like her child, he still wasn't comfortable with the thought of having one of his own.

She shouldn't have felt that sharp little pain at the thought. After all, she'd already walked this route. But then, this was her son. She wanted everyone to want him.

Not everyone would, though, she knew. It was just a fact of life, one she still struggled with.

"All right, ready to meet the family?" she asked, striving for brightness.

He placed a restraining hand on her bare arm, sending warmth and awareness straight into her. "Not a chance I'm going to drag you into this." His expression was stern.

She couldn't help the look of confusion that crossed her face.

He shrugged and smiled. "What I mean is, thank you for the ride, but I accepted because Fiona said that you were going, anyway, and because I wanted to make sure that the jerk who attacked you earlier didn't follow you. He hasn't. But now that we're here, I'm not dragging you into this any deeper. The Carsons are obviously your friends. Furthermore, they don't have any more reason to like me than I have reason to like them. In fact, they have every reason to be suspicious of me and to order me out of here. I might as well tell you that their suspicions would not be without grounds. I'm not a violent man unless someone's being threatened, but I'm not likely to feel too kindly toward the family that made my mother's life a joke and a humiliation. So you and I part ways for now. Go circulate, Cinderella. Just be careful. Not all men—"

"—are trustworthy. I know," she said with a smile. "A wise man told me that earlier this evening."

He rubbed his jaw. "Check back with me on that 'wise man' thing at the end of the evening. You might change your mind."

She hoped she'd changed her mind about some things, because right now Ace Carson looked very much like a man she wanted to kiss. And she had the feeling his kisses would be very difficult to forget.

What in hell was he doing here? The question played through Ace's mind again and again as he located Fiona and followed her across the lobby of the main building of the Lone Star Country Club, an impressive structure that stretched up four stories. She led him into the elegant blue-and-ivory Empire Room, one of several dining rooms that were apparently available. The whole place smelled like luxury, redolent with flowers and the colognes of the well-heeled men and women who mingled here.

My mother might have cleaned some of their houses at one time, he couldn't help thinking. She would never have been invited here. He almost felt like a traitor for even stepping through the door, but then, of course, it was because of his mother he was here. Once he'd known the whole truth, he'd had to come. For her. And he was pretty darn sure that wherever she was, she was looking down on him right now. It was time he won back a bit of the pride that had been stolen from her.

"Okay, you ready?" Fiona looked up at Ace. He shrugged and couldn't help searching the perimeters of the room for Crystal.

His little half sister laughed lightly. "She's watching from the shadows. I have the feeling that Crystal is waiting to come in and save you if need be. She told me what you did. She doesn't like to feel obligated to anyone."

"She doesn't need to feel obligated."

Fiona raised her brows. "You don't know Crystal."

No, he didn't, and it would probably be best if he didn't get to know her any better. The fact that she drew his attention like nectar attracted hummingbirds should have already told him he needed to back away. So when he sensed her presence over in the corner, he tried not to look in her direction.

He failed, and he saw that she was in conversation with a smiling, sandy-haired man.

"Ace." Fiona's voice slipped in.

"He's what? He's who?" a loud, angry male voice at his elbow demanded.

Ace forced his attention away from Crystal and turned toward the angry voice. A man frowned at him. No, make that two men and a woman. The men were both tall, with brown hair, and blue eyes like his. The woman, with her dark brown hair and green eyes, was almost a mirror image of Fiona. The men looked grim, the woman uncertain.

"Are you sure he's related to us?" one man asked, ignoring Ace.

Fiona turned toward Ace. "Not completely, no, but look at his eyes. They're a lot like yours, Matt, and enough like Flynt's that there has to be some Carson blood in him."

The woman who resembled Fiona closed her eyes for a second, as if she was wishing him away. When she opened her eyes again, she blinked once and nodded.

"I'm Cara," she said. "Fiona's twin, as you can see, and my sister said your name was what?" She looked as if she really didn't want to know, but good manners obliged her to ask.

Ace raised a brow. "Ace Turner Carson," he said slowly.

"What do you want?" There was no welcome in the older brother's voice.

"Flynt..." Fiona drawled a warning.

But Ace just smiled, a long slow smile. He *wanted* to make people uneasy. "I don't want much," he said truthfully. "I'm not here to stake a claim, if that's what you mean, little brother."

"But you want something or you wouldn't be here," the younger brother stated.

"That's Matt," Cara said. "And he has a point."

"He does. Everyone wants something, after all, don't they?" Ace asked. "I suppose the Carsons—all of you—want to protect your money and your name."

"You say that as if you mean to threaten us in some way," Flynt accused, but he looked slightly less hostile now, as if the shock had had time to settle. "Is that what you're here to do?"

Not exactly.

"I don't want any of the Carson cash," Ace said, biting off the words, "and believe me, I don't pose a threat to any of the Carsons' health. Wouldn't *you* come looking if you found out you had relatives you never knew about?"

The two men seemed to be wrestling with that concept. Fiona and Cara exchanged a look.

"Branson Hines was bothering Crystal tonight. He tried to force her to kiss him. Ace stepped in and sent him packing," Fiona said softly.

Matt and Flynt Carson looked at each other. Flynt's lips twisted slightly, as he seemed to study what little information he'd been given. Not that Ace cared. He wasn't looking for anyone's blessing. In fact, it was the last thing he wanted or needed. He started to walk away.

"Carson."

At the single word, Ace stopped and turned back. Flynt's blue eyes were narrowed. "Let's get one thing straight," he said. "I don't like you and I don't like you being here, but I hope you broke his nose."

Ace rubbed his jaw. "Afraid not. I'm not an especially violent man." His voice sounded cold and barely restrained even to his own ears.

"He nearly choked him," Fiona volunteered.

"Um, I see, not violent," Matt noted with a frown.

"Didn't appear that he was going to go away without some persuasion," Ace admitted.

"And you persuaded him?" Cara asked.

"It's something I'm good at."

The two men exchanged a look.

"You planning on being around real long?" Matt asked.

"For a while."

"I take it you aren't expecting a big welcome?"

"That would be a bit out of place. And unwarranted since I'm not exactly here on a quest to mend fallen fences." He stared into his younger half brother's eyes and saw a bit of himself looking back. He didn't like the feeling it gave him. He realized that he had the advantage. He'd come here knowing that there were untold secrets on the Carson front. The four Carson brothers and sisters were just facing that fact.

"If you'll excuse me," Ace said, and he nodded and turned to leave again.

"You still haven't told us, Ace, what your intentions are in coming here,'' Fiona said, and when he looked at her, she didn't look as much worried as speculative. Out of the corner of his eye he saw Crystal. She was watching him, and her eyes were big with worry.

"Hell," he said almost beneath his breath.

"Pardon me?" Cara said.

A smile lifted the corners of Ace's mouth. He looked at the expensively dressed, obviously privileged group standing before him. He couldn't forget the innocent woman standing off to the side worrying, and he knew he'd been right all along. He didn't fit in here and never would. But then, he hadn't come here for that; he hadn't even come to stay very long at all. He *had* come here for a reason.

"I just came to raise a little hell like I always have," he told Cara, and smiled as she blinked. "I regret to inform you, baby sister, that your oldest brother doesn't care much about pomp or prestige or the joys of settling down and behaving himself. And I'm here just to meet the clan, let you know I exist and who I am. And then, in time, when I've caused enough talk and trouble and discomfort, I'll do what all men like me tend to do. Drift away. Move on. And you can go on as you always have. Except you'll know that there's one more Carson out there. Hell, you'll wonder, like I do, just how many more of us there actually are. Now I think I'll move along. Nice meeting all of you Carsons."

And he saluted his half brothers and sisters and strode off.

As he passed the part of the room where he'd last seen Crystal, Ace couldn't help looking her way. He was on his way—for the first time in his life—to face the man who had seduced his mother, contributed his DNA and then turned his back forever on her and the son he'd fathered. He should have been elated, gleeful even. It was the moment Ace had prepared for, maybe all his life.

But instead of joy, he felt as if concrete weights were pressing on him.

He should have been clipping across the floor on his way to deliver the news to his father that the "bad penny" Carson had just shown up. Instead, he moved to Crystal like steel to magnet. He looked down at the complete concern in her big hazel eyes, and a low groan escaped him.

She was leaning against a wall, hovering in the background, staring at him as if he were Timmy or some other soul in need of her concern. It occurred to him that she was genuinely worried about him. That wouldn't do. She had enough grief in her life. She didn't need to be thinking about *his* problems.

Somehow he managed a teasing smile. He leaned one palm against the wall and swooped in close.

"You, darlin', are driving me completely nuts tonight," he whispered right next to her ear.

He felt the shiver slide through her. She lifted her chin. "What do you mean?"

Ace gave her his best slow lazy smile, designed to disarm and chase away ugly worrisome thoughts. "I mean that the whole time I was talking to the gang," he said, nodding in the direction where the Carson siblings were still standing deep in conversation, "I kept thinking that I wanted to do this."

And with one fluid motion, he slid his arm lightly around her waist. He slipped his other hand beneath her hair and exposed her neck to his view. Lightly he touched his lips to the spot where her pulse was pounding. He gave her plenty of time to slither away, plenty of room to run.

Instead, she gasped softly. If anything, she moved closer.

He closed his eyes, afraid to move. Had he meant to scare her? No, definitely not, but maybe he'd meant to warn her that she shouldn't trust him any more than that Branson character. That she shouldn't waste her worry on a man like him who could not stick around any more than Timmy's father had.

"Are you worried about meeting Ford?" she whispered.

He shook his head. "No." The word came out a little harshly. And hell, why not? With Crystal's body this close, what man wouldn't feel like he was losing control? "No," he said more softly.

But when he pulled back, he saw that he hadn't soothed her a bit. If anything, she looked more concerned about him than ever.

And when he turned and walked away, he thought he heard her soft steps behind him.

Five

Crystal followed along a good ten feet behind Ace, unable to stop herself. She'd watched him with his newly found half brothers and sisters. She'd seen the way he'd handled the situation, playing it light, but there was something rigid about his jaw. He stood apart. Because he disliked them or because he expected them to dislike him?

He had obviously come to meet the family, but he just as obviously had no desire to linger. He didn't appear to have any love for his father; he spoke of revenge for someone other than himself, but insisted he wasn't a violent man.

Ace Carson was a million questions wrapped into a couple of great big questions. Who was he really and why was he here?

She didn't have a clue who he was, but his touch had made her want to turn in his arms and press against him. He insisted he wasn't respectable, but he had protected her twice.

She had a feeling he was good at protecting other people, but who was going to protect him? He was moving across the room to meet the man who had not wanted him even when he was an innocent, appealing baby. What must that be like?

For a moment a vision of her own son doing this same thing, seeking out his father years from now, rose before her, and her heart nearly cracked.

But she looked at Ace. He wasn't like Timmy and he was a very strong man, yet right now he was about as alone in this town as a man could be.

She walked on behind him.

Then from a side door, she sensed a presence. Crystal turned to see Ford Carson moving toward them with his thick white hair, his bushy eyebrows and his air of complete command. People approached him, eager to speak to this towering man they all knew and loved so well, but he shook his head and kept moving toward Ace.

Like an animal sniffing the air for danger, Ace stopped suddenly. He turned and saw his father for the first time.

For several seconds he didn't move. Then he frowned and stepped forward. He glanced at Crystal out of the corner of his eye. For a moment, she thought he was going to tell her that it wasn't safe for her to be here. She probably shouldn't be intruding like this, but she wasn't sure she could let him do this alone. Again the image of Timmy doing the same thing rose before her. Again she realized that Ace wasn't Timmy, but still, she had to stay.

And in spite of the tension of the moment, Ace seemed to understand. He winked at her and motioned her to a nearby table. An audience of one.

Crystal prepared to do what she'd come to do. If only she knew what that was. For now she simply watched and waited as Ford and Ace met not quite twenty feet from her.

"Someone told me there was a man looking for me. A stranger. Since you're the only stranger I see here, and you look as if you're looking for someone, I'm assuming you're the man everyone is talking about," Ford said. He stood there, handsome as all the Carsons were, with the height he'd bequeathed to all his sons and a barely suppressed air of expectation. Due to a heart condition that had flared up again recently, he looked like an aging gunfighter, tired, wary, but a little excited at the danger and still able to command power and send fear racing through his opponents when he needed to.

"I guess maybe I am that man," Ace said, moving forward, his steps sure and deliberate.

"Then I guess I'd like to know what you want."

"Not much." Ace gazed steadily at Ford. His stance was relaxed, even casual, but Crystal saw that his hands were bunched into fists. "I just came to pass on some news to you."

"You're not from around here."

"No, about two hundred miles away. West. Hampsted."

She thought she saw Ford drag in a breath. Surely Fiona or Flynt had warned him what was coming. If so, why didn't he just say so? But then it occurred to her that this might not be a new experience for him. He might have gone through something like this before. A man like Ford, with his money and prestige, probably had people making claims on him all the time. False claims.

Crystal almost closed her eyes at that thought. Her heart felt as if it stopped much too long to keep her blood flowing. She looked straight at Ace and saw that he was studying her, not Ford, at that moment. She wondered what he was thinking, if he was questioning her the way she was questioning him.

But she wasn't really questioning him. Anyone who saw the two men standing together could never deny that they were related. Ace wasn't a false prophet. He smiled at her and gave her an encouraging nod as if to tell her that he was just sharing a beer with an old friend and would be right over to kiss her and take her home any minute now. "Not much longer, darlin'," his eyes seemed to say.

"What's the news you've brought me?" Ford asked, and his voice was slightly unsteady.

"Just that an old friend of yours passed away. You might not really remember her. Her name was Rebecca. Rebecca Barron originally. It was a long time ago that she knew you. She just asked me to stop by, so I said I would."

He said this casually, as if he barely knew the woman in question, though it was clear to Crystal that the woman had been his mother.

Ford's hands were bunched into fists now, but he didn't respond to Ace's suggestion that he might have either known or forgotten the woman. "Do you live in Hampsted?" he asked, instead.

"Sometimes. I'm not big on roots, though."

For half a second, Crystal thought she saw fierce intent in Ace's eyes, but then she blinked and decided she was wrong, because he was wearing that long, slow, I-don't-give-a-damn-about-anything smile.

"I see. Are you…just passing through Mission Creek?"

"I am. But first I'm going to stay and see the sights and have a little fun."

His tone implied that there would be drinking and brawling and women involved. Crystal tried not to dwell on that.

"You have a place to stay, son?" Ford's voice dipped low, almost coming out as a choked whisper.

"I'm fine," Ace said a bit too quickly. "I've rented rooms at the Overton Apartments."

Crystal heard a soft gasp at her side and she looked up to see Cara standing beside her. "That's a hell-hole," Cara whispered, as if Crystal didn't already know that. Everybody did. "Nola Warburn rents out rooms by the hour sometimes, and I don't even want to think how seldom the sheets get changed."

In the silence that had followed Ace's statement, Cara's whisper carried.

A smile played over Ace's lips, and Crystal knew that he was as aware of Nola Warburn's reputation as everyone else was.

"I can find you a better place," Ford said.

"That's very kind, but where I'm at is just fine. It suits me. I won't be there long, anyway."

"No one ever is," Fiona said. Obviously the entire Carson crowd had arrived. Even Grace, Ford's wife, was watching carefully from beside her children. She didn't move forward. Of course. She was the woman that Ford *had* married. She probably hadn't known about Ace's mother.

Crystal gave Grace a worried look. Pretty and plump and blond, she was naturally pale, but today she was even paler than usual. Still, she was hanging in there. And she was looking at Ace with sad eyes.

Ace gave everyone a smile and a slight bow. "If you'll excuse me, it's late, and you have a party to see to," he said. "And I'm a workingman. Got to get up early."

A look of confusion passed over Ford's features. "I thought you weren't staying."

"I'm not, but a man has to eat. I usually find work in most places I visit. In sales, usually. If any one of you needs a good luxury car, you be sure to stop over at Mission Creek Motors. I'd be happy to fit you out with the best that money can buy.

"Nice meeting all of you. Ma'am," he said, turning to Grace and tilting his head in a careful salute of goodbye as he moved away.

"Mission Creek Motors?" Flynt said, and gave a low whistle. "Hell and more hell, Dad. You've gone and fathered a son who intends to run you out of the car business."

For the first time in the course of the conversation, Ford almost smiled. "Looks like you're right about that. I'd say that he's not exactly happy to have discovered he's my son."

Grace came up and touched her husband gently on the arm. "It's more than that, Ford."

He looked at her with bleak eyes. "I know, and

I'm sorry. Let's go home, love. It's been a long day. Too much to think about for one night.''

"By tomorrow we'll have a plan," she assured him, kissing his cheek as they walked away.

Fiona turned to Crystal. "Do you think he really means to run Daddy's dealership out of town?"

Matt gave her a look of disbelief. "Lone Star Auto has been in business much longer than Mission Creek Motors, and we've always pulled in more sales than J.D. has."

"Yes, but J.D. was in it just for fun. Ace Carson is looking for blood and payback."

"The women will probably flock there," Cara said, looking at Crystal. Crystal felt her face flame.

"He's just a man I met today," she said softly. "He helped me when I needed it. He's leaving when he's done whatever he plans to do."

"He plans to get some of his own back from the Carsons, it looks like," Matt said. "Might do it, too. Can you imagine what people are thinking? A Carson living in the Overton Apartments and selling the competitor's cars?" His voice was indignant, but before he'd finished speaking, he began to grin and shake his head. "Things have been a bit tame around here lately," he said. "This could prove interesting."

Cara frowned. "Daddy's upset. He's always been in control of everything."

Fiona nodded. "Well, it looks like this is one man he can't control. I wonder if there's a woman who can tame Ace Carson," she said, smiling at Crystal.

Her comment made Crystal's breath catch. She remembered how it had felt when Ace had placed his hand on her waist, his lips against her skin.

She stood. "Like the man said, I have to work tomorrow. And Timmy needs his own bed."

Fiona smiled, but Crystal raised her brows and held up a hand. "This topic is off-limits, Fiona. There's too much we don't know here, and too much we'll probably never know. I'm leaving now. I'm going home. My own home," she stressed, "and I would appreciate it if you would get those matchmaking notions right out of your head."

Fiona lifted one delicate shoulder. Her husband, Clay, and Cara's husband, Omar, came up behind them. Clay looped an arm around his wife and Omar kissed Cara's cheek.

"Have our wives been causing trouble for you, Crystal?" Omar asked.

Crystal smiled at the men, who were so obviously in love. "Just the usual. Fiona's trying to marry me off to every man that comes down the pike."

"Not just any man this time," Fiona said as Crystal waved and walked away.

"Not by a long shot," Crystal whispered to herself. Ace Turner was a maddening, sensual, gloriously attractive man with a protective streak for women that was bigger than the town of Mission Creek, and he was about as easy to hold on to as air. It was time to stop thinking about him.

But when she walked out the door of the Lone Star Country Club leading Timmy by the hand, Ace was waiting there, leaning against the porch rail, his arms crossed.

He smiled when he saw her.

"I thought you'd gone," she said.

"You're my ride," he told her. "And I believe the saying holds here. You leave the dance with the one who brought you."

She shook her head and chuckled. "I believe that applies to dating practices. We're not dating."

"No, ma'am, and not likely to be, either." But when he took her hand to lead her and Timmy through the dark parking lot, his hand was warm and strong and it took all the power she possessed to remind herself that he was just doing her a kindness. After all, Ace was a car salesman. He probably had any number of vehicles at his disposal.

When they got to her car and opened the door, the light poured out, revealing a long key scratch on the side. An involuntary gasp escaped Crystal's lips.

"Hell," Ace said.

Automatically Crystal's fingers skimmed the ugly gouge. It was only a car, but it was hers, and this had obviously been an intentional act of destruction. She picked Timmy up and pulled him close in a protective embrace.

"Who would do this?" she asked. Who would have anything against her? The answer came to her. Branson.

"Don't think about it," Ace said, his voice tight with leashed anger. "Come on, let's get you home. I'll drive."

"Should we report it?"

"Yes, but tomorrow will be soon enough. Whoever did this is most likely gone."

Or watching.

But she saw Ace looking at Timmy and she had to agree. Even if someone was watching, they could not attend to the problem right now. Not while her child was at risk.

They drove in silence, Ace's hands tense on the wheel, Crystal's mind tumbling like a tornado blowing through the town. Only Timmy was peaceful as the motion of the car lulled him into dreamland.

"This isn't the way to the Overton Apartments. This is the way to my house."

"Fancy that," he said.

"You're coming home with me?" Her voice felt strange and stiff and slightly panicked. The thought of Ace Turner Carson in her house or even near her house, taking up the space, filling it with his overwhelming presence, was almost too much for her to contemplate.

He shook his head. "Relax, darlin', I'm just escorting you home. I'll leave when we get there."

"How? You said that I was your ride."

"I lied. And don't worry about how. I've been getting around on my own since I was old enough to think for myself."

She wondered what that meant. What had his childhood been like? How different had it been from that of his half brothers and sisters?

Crystal turned to him, studying the way the shadows and streetlights turned his handsome face even more handsome and mysterious.

"You stayed and waited for me because you

thought Branson might come looking for me, didn't you," she said.

"Not necessarily."

"Not necessarily?"

He shook his head, as if shaking off his own thoughts. "He wasn't happy when he left. He obviously still had things he wanted to say. There was reason to believe that he might come here to let off a little more steam. That was one reason I stayed."

"What was the other one?"

He took one hand off the wheel. He lifted her hair and cupped his palm around her neck, his thumb stroking the spot he'd kissed earlier.

She swallowed hard. "I can't."

"I know. I can't, either, but you and Timmy needed an escort, and I needed a few moments of peace talking to a sweet woman, something to lull me asleep at Nola Warburn's place."

"I hear Nola can provide cures for insomnia," she teased.

He turned to her and smiled. "You ever been there, darlin'?"

Her grin grew. "As a matter of fact, I have."

He raised a brow. "I don't believe you."

"Believe me. Nola and I went to school together. I sneaked off there once after school to play. My mother came and dragged me home, but not before Nola taught me her secret."

Ace frowned. "Her secret?"

"The way to drive a man wild."

Ace's fingers froze on her skin. "How old were you?"

"Old enough."

"And what's the secret?" he asked. He had pulled up to her house and had turned to her. She noticed the cab waiting across the street, one he must have called for before they left the country club. He must have discovered where she lived then, too. He'd planned ahead. She wondered what else he'd planned when he'd decided to come to Mission Creek.

"The secret to driving a man wild," she said with a small smile, "is never give him what he really wants."

"Well, then, that shouldn't be too tough. I have a strong feeling that what I want is something you can't give me."

"And what's that? What do you want?"

He got out of the car. He circled around and opened Timmy's door and removed the sleeping child. Then he opened Crystal's door and drew her out. He walked her to her door, waited until she'd unlocked her house and switched on the light. Then he placed Timmy in her arms and smiled.

She gazed up at him. "You didn't answer my question. What are you really here for? What do you want?"

He stared down into her eyes and touched her cheek. "I don't want anything. There's nothing in the town of Mission Creek that I want, and you, my sweet little hospital fund-raiser, are a woman who wants a lot of something in your life."

She frowned and shook her head fiercely. "I don't want anything from you."

"I didn't say you did, but you do want something.

You have a child. He has needs, and that means you have needs, whether you like it or not. You want things, Crystal. You definitely do, but the last thing you want is what a man like me can give you.''

He bent his head, gave her a quick hard kiss and then gently nudged her inside the door.

"Lock it. Now," he said, and she did as she was told. Dazed and shaken by his touch, she could do nothing else. She needed to put some distance between them. A closed door at the very least.

But as she heard the door of the cab close, heard the engine roar as the car pulled away, she sank down with Timmy, holding him close and safe in her arms. She swept her fingers across her lips where Ace had warmed them and made them ache.

She wanted him to touch her again. Kiss her again.

The very thought scared her, because he was right. She might not want to ever marry, but she had needs. What she needed most in her life was stability. For herself and for her son. Especially for her son.

But there was no question in her mind that the man who had just kissed her didn't have a high regard for or need for stability. He lived for the moment. When he took a woman in his arms, he took her passion and then moved on to the next woman.

She'd have to be the worst kind of fool to get caught up in that.

And she had been a fool too many times.

"I don't want you, Ace," she whispered out loud.

But she knew that was a lie. She wanted him. Right here. Right now. His lips against hers. Again.

* * *

It seemed he'd been living in the shadows most of his life, Branson Hines thought from his position across the street beneath the trees. He liked the darkness.

It enabled him to find out what was going on, to get close to people without them knowing it. His eyesight after dark was excellent. That came in handy sometimes.

Like tonight.

He'd gotten away from those security guards easily enough. And he'd seen that witch and her kid, seen how she'd let the man kiss her when she'd refused Branson's kiss earlier.

"She always survives," he muttered. In spite of what he'd told everyone about her years ago, look what had happened. She'd become the hospital fundraiser and the darling of the Carsons. In spite of being a total slut, she had a little boy—unlike his sweet wife, Deena, who'd lost her baby when she'd stepped into that hospital, that place of evil.

"Not fair, not nearly fair," he said.

But he would make it fair. Oh, yes, he would. Crystal Bennett's luck couldn't hold out forever.

Six

Had a woman's lips ever tasted so sweet? It was the first thought that edged into Ace's thoughts the next morning when he woke up—and he didn't like it.

"Get her out of your mind, Carson," he told himself, closing his eyes and attempting to reclaim the relative oblivion of sleep.

Didn't work. All he could see were big hazel eyes. All he could remember was the softness of her skin, the dazed, desire-filled look in her eyes when he'd pulled back.

Crystal had blinked and recovered quickly. She'd colored up prettily, and he could see that she was no doubt counting herself lucky that he had more or less told her he wasn't staying around and would leave her alone.

But he still wanted to gaze into her eyes as he slipped into her body. He wanted to hear her gasp and cry out with satisfaction.

Knowing that he would do none of those things didn't make the need less intense.

"Time for an icy shower, buddy," he told himself, forcing himself from bed and into the bathroom. "Get her out of your mind. She's been hurt by men before and she doesn't want that again. Besides, she has a boy. A very little boy. Innocent and vulnerable. A boy who hasn't yet learned that people can be fickle, that they can hurt him when he hasn't done anything wrong.'' Boys like that blamed themselves when things went wrong. They smiled, and you smiled back. And when you left, they wondered if they'd done something wrong and what it was. Soon their smiles came less often and then not at all. They ceased to trust.

A boy that young should still be able to trust.

A woman that pure of heart should be able to leave her house without worrying that some man with lustful intentions would take advantage of her goodness and her warmth and her loveliness.

She wasn't going to have to worry about him. He was going to stick around only long enough to be an annoyance to Ford, long enough to remind him and his that there were at least some consequences for every action, even those that had happened long ago.

Then he would finally feel as if he'd done a little something for his mother, given back a tiny bit of what had been taken from her. And then he would go, leaving Crystal Bennett as innocent as he'd found her.

It was some kind of a plan, at least.

As he felt some of the morning's tension ease and made his way to the kitchen, the phone rang.

''Yeah?'' He held the receiver between his shoulder and ear as he opened the door to the beat-up refrigerator and stared at a lot of nothing.

''Hmm, grumpy in the morning. Not specifically a

Carson trait, but interesting." It was Fiona's too-cheerful voice.

"I assume you have a reason for calling."

"Maybe I just wanted to make sure Crystal got home safely last night."

"You could have called her to ask that."

"I wonder. I saw her leave with you. She might have told me if Branson was bothering her again, but I'm not sure she would have discussed you with me even if you were less than a gentleman."

"I'm not a gentleman and there's nothing to discuss." But her words gave him pause.

He'd seen the worried look in Crystal's eyes when he'd gone to see Ford last night. He hadn't missed the fact that she'd taken his hand. To protect him? Fiona was right. Crystal wouldn't complain about his behavior to a Carson.

"She's fine," he said a bit too roughly. "At least she was when I left her."

"Might be a good idea to call and find out for sure, though. Just in case Branson rang her doorbell after you left."

He was way ahead of her on that one. And like it or not, determined to keep his distance from Crystal or not, he intended to make sure Branson left her alone.

"Good point. Is there anything else?" he asked. "I'm just getting ready for work."

"Oh, yes, Mission Creek Motors. You could probably have a job at Lone Star Auto, you know."

No, he couldn't. He had lived his whole life at the wealthy academy where his mother had ended up working, fighting the accusations that he wanted to be an interloper, a climber, a pretender, a wanna-be who didn't really belong at the school. It had taken him years to fight free. He was done with that. And this was just more of the same.

The distance between him and the Carsons was glaring enough. He'd come here to show Ford that he'd survived in spite of everything and didn't need the big bad Carsons to help him succeed. He'd come here to show Ford Carson he could give him a run for his money, even make him a little uncomfortable. Doing the nine-to-five under the thumb of Ford Carson would give Ford the power. And the old man had already exercised his power over Ace—and his mother. Ace didn't want to be one of *the* Carsons of Mission Creek. And he sure didn't want anyone thinking differently.

"I don't think I'd be a good match for Lone Star Auto. I like it just fine where I am. Now if you'll excuse me…"

"Sure, I was just going, but…"

"Yes?"

"There *is* one thing."

He waited.

"I was just wondering…I thought…well, Clay and I are having a little dinner party here later. Perhaps you'd like to bring Crystal."

It was the last thing Ace had expected to hear.

"You want me to come to dinner?"

"With Crystal."

Ah, now he was getting it. He remembered a few times last night when Fiona had appeared to get a certain look in her eyes. A born matchmaker, he guessed. Not a shy one, either. And her aim right now was to match Crystal with the new man in town. He was a little disappointed in Fiona. Surely she remembered what he'd told her about where he was staying and what he was doing while he was here, neither of which made him look like much of a catch. He wondered what the other men she'd tried to set Crystal up with had been like—and found he didn't really want to know.

"I don't think that's a good idea."

"Because you don't want to have dinner with the Carsons, or because you don't want me to fix you up with Crystal?"

He wasn't prepared to answer. He doubted he *could* answer if he tried.

"When I make a date with a woman, I prefer to do my own planning," he finally said, his excuse sounding lame even to his own ears.

"Hmm, well, I just thought it would be one way to keep her safe while Branson is in this mood."

"Is he truly dangerous?"

"Could be. He's served time in jail, but not for anything violent. Still, he went berserk after his wife, Deena, lost her baby when she went into premature labor. And he has an ugly history with Crystal, but that was a long time ago. I'm not sure why he targeted her yesterday."

Which meant the man was unpredictable. It was already obvious he was unstable. Fiona was right— someone needed to keep an eye on Crystal. For the next few days, at any rate.

"Hmm," he said.

"Exactly," Fiona replied. "You'll come to dinner?"

"I told you, I like to do things my own way when I'm getting involved with a woman."

"And are you planning on getting involved with her?" He could almost hear the satisfaction in Fiona's voice.

"I'm just going to make sure Branson doesn't think she's fair game. I'll be a presence."

"I like that."

"Don't like it too much. It won't last, and you should be grateful for that. Crystal is destined for someone a lot more domestic than I am."

"She doesn't want to get married. I know that much."

He did, too, but for some reason it grated coming from someone else. What did Crystal do? Advertise to the entire world that she wasn't available to any man?

"It won't come to that," he promised. "This will be short and simple. More of a task than a relationship," he assured his half sister.

But he had to admit, when he had hung up the phone, it was a task that might be pleasant. Crystal was an appetizing woman, and he was feeling rather hungry at the moment. As long as both of them recognized that they didn't want to let things go too far, why shouldn't they at least get to know each other a little?

Crystal hung up the phone and wondered when Fiona would stop trying to fix her up with every man who entered her field of vision.

She hadn't even bothered to try to hide the fact that she was matchmaking.

"Fiona," Crystal had said, "doesn't it bother you that Ace is obviously here to settle some kind of score with your family? Your father in particular?"

"Yes, it bothers me a lot."

"Then why do you want me to date him?"

"Hmm, I don't know. Maybe because I don't believe that anyone can really resist the Carson clan?" she teased. "Or because if you married him, you and I would be related?" Crystal could almost imagine Fiona's grin.

"Not exactly the most stable basis for a marriage, sweetie," Crystal reminded her friend.

"Maybe not, and maybe I'll regret trying to throw you two together, but he protected you. You don't get enough of that. You try to convince everyone that you don't need anyone, and it sends most men running."

"That's the idea. And I *don't* need anyone."

"You have to admit that he's a looker."

"He's a Carson. You're all lookers. And looks don't make for a stable relationship, either. I had that with John. He even looked good walking away."

"He *ran* away. Coward."

"Yes."

"And it wasn't you he was running from. It was fatherhood."

"And marriage. And Ace doesn't want marriage, either, in case you don't know that."

"Yes, well, I can guess. He doesn't look like he's thinking of domestic chores when he turns those blue eyes on you. Although he does look a bit like he's imagining activities related to babies.''

Crystal didn't know what to say. ''You really think that no one can resist the Carson clan?'' She wondered if she was thinking about Ace resisting Fiona's friendliness, or herself resisting Ace's bedroom looks.

''I guess you'll see. He's on his way over to see you before work. Why don't you bring him over to my house for dinner tonight?''

''If you know that he's on his way over here, then you must have talked to him. I can only assume that he turned down your offer of a meal.''

''Stubborn man.''

''Yes, and he's going to stay that way. I am not going to begin dating your half brother or any other man who looks like something so sinful he should be poured over ice cream. I've told you a thousand times I'm strictly into simple friendly relationships with men from here on out.''

''Well, it was worth a try.'' Fiona let out a long sigh.

Crystal wasn't going to rise to the bait. She was going to hang up just as soon as she found out one thing. ''Why exactly is Ace on his way over here?''

''Maybe because he just can't stay away,'' Fiona suggested.

''Or because you told him something that sent him over here,'' Crystal guessed.

''That, too,'' Fiona admitted. ''But you can ask him about it when he gets there.'' And then she hung up.

Now Crystal was standing in the middle of the room trying to decide what to do. She wasn't due at the hospital for another hour and so she hadn't gotten dressed yet. Her hair was still loose and slightly mussed from a night in bed, and her pale blue sleep shirt had seen many washings and clung to her curves the way old soft shirts do. Her feet were bare. Worse, she hadn't yet had coffee or anything else to brace her for the next few minutes.

What she needed was a backbone. What she did not need was to have to face Ace when her lips were still tingling from his kiss the night before.

But the doorbell rang at that moment and it didn't matter what she needed. What she had was one gorgeous man standing on her doorstep.

She let him in. His gaze shifted immediately to her bare legs. He didn't look even vaguely apologetic. No surprise. Women probably spent hours dreaming up ways to show him their legs. Most women would probably consider her lucky.

Crystal tried to nonchalantly cross her arms—and her legs.

Ace grinned. "It's not working, you know. You still look like something a man is supposed to find in his bed if he's incredibly lucky."

Warmth stole up from her toes to the top of her head. It traveled back down through her body, stopping in all the places that made her aware that she was a woman and Ace Carson was a man.

"Can I help you?" she finally managed to ask, not sure where to start.

He shook his head. "Fiona suggested that Branson

might have made a repeat visit to your side after I left last night. I just wanted to make sure you were all right.''

She didn't want to be touched by his concern. But darn it, what was a woman supposed to do when he just stood there looking as if he really was concerned about more than her legs?

''I haven't seen him since you chased him away,'' she replied.

''Good. I'll try to keep it that way.''

She blinked. ''Which means what?''

He shrugged. ''I'm here for a short while. My job isn't that demanding. I can make myself useful while I'm in Mission Creek. Any problems with that?''

Yes, more problems than she cared to examine if he meant what it sounded like he meant. ''What did Fiona say to you?''

''Fiona thinks you and I should get to know each other better.''

''Fiona is sometimes too…helpful for her own good, but she's also skipping down the wrong path.''

''I know that. So does she, I think.''

His easy compliance should have offered her some relief. Instead, it stung.

''Don't get me wrong. Fiona's a good person,'' Crystal said.

Ace didn't answer.

''She's a wonderful person, actually.''

He stared at her, his lips even curved in a smile slightly, but he didn't comment.

''You'll like her once you get to know her. She's

very special," Crystal continued somewhat defensively.

"Crystal," Ace drawled, "you don't have to do this. In fact, it would be best if you didn't do this."

"Do what?"

"Attempt to patch things up between my sister and me."

"What's to patch up? You don't even know each other. I'm only saying that if you got to know each other—"

"We won't."

"Would you like to have dinner at her house?" Where had that come from? Hadn't she just told Fiona that this dinner thing wasn't going to happen?

"I'm sorry, but I just don't do the small cozy dinner circuit. Too uncomfortable. I'm not here to make peace with the Carsons, Crystal."

"They're family."

"Not mine."

And there was something in his voice that warned her not to take this any further. She supposed he was right. She didn't know a thing about him. She had no right to judge or to press.

"Nice suit," she said, instead, and smiled. He was dressed in crisp black and white. "Not exactly typical auto-showroom attire."

"J.D. wants everything about the place to say formal, expensive, luxurious. At least that's what he told me."

She knew that. She'd been by J.D.'s place, but she could have told the owner that none of the other salesmen even began to fill out a suit the way Ace did.

Most of his salesmen looked like funeral directors in their stark black and white. Ace, however, looked all man—and a terribly attractive one, at that. Still...

"You need just a touch of color, something that hints at a bit of adventure. Wait here," she told him.

She left the room, then came back with a deep maroon scarf. Carefully she folded it and stepped close to Ace. She tried her best not to breathe in the clean male scent of him or to notice that his shoulders were broad and his chest was, too. Something was definitely wrong with her, because she was not a morning person, yet this morning all her senses were on full alert. She had a strong desire to slip her hands beneath the lapels of Ace's jacket and slide it off him as she kissed her way down the stark white of his shirt.

She hoped beyond hope that she wasn't blushing. "There," she said, tucking the scarf into his pocket and finishing up somewhat clumsily. "Now you look just a little bit different, a little bit bolder than usual. You'll attract attention."

As if he wouldn't have before. Ace Turner Carson would attract attention if he were clad in...well, in anything. Or in nothing.

"That's what I came here to do," he said softly, placing a finger beneath her chin. "I came to attract attention."

Crystal felt as if her skin was on fire. She felt as if she would die for lack of air if he didn't lean down and kiss her. He was certainly attracting her attention.

"After you've gotten everyone's attention, then what will you do?" she asked.

"Then I'll leave," he said simply and solemnly,

looking straight into her eyes as he said it. "I'll leave, Crystal." She knew he was telling her something very important. Don't be like my mother. Don't follow the path you followed once before. Don't make a mistake about a man who has no intention of being here when hard times strike. Be true to yourself and yourself alone.

"Well," she said, looking at her watch, "if you're going to leave, then you'd better leave soon. Mission Creek Motors opens in ten minutes."

He swore beneath his breath and looked at his own watch.

"Do not let Branson Hines get too near you today," he said.

She looked up at him as if he'd just told her not to jump off any high cliffs. "Do I look that gullible?"

"Yes," he said, causing her to gasp. "I can see what's in your eyes, Crystal. I'm betting that if he apologized and told you that he'd made a mistake yesterday, you'd forgive him. You'd let down your guard. Don't."

"You think I'm a pushover."

"I think you see things in people that aren't there," he said. And he leaned over as if he was going to kiss her goodbye again.

He didn't. Instead, he pulled back, and she saw that he wasn't looking at her anymore. He was looking beyond her.

"Hey, wildcat, you have a great day today, do you hear? Make your mom laugh."

Timmy giggled, his pudgy cheeks dimpling. "Jokes," he agreed. "Benny told me some."

"Uh-oh," Crystal said.

"Uh-oh?" Ace raised a brow.

"Benny is learning to swear. At age three," she said, unable to keep the incredulity or concern from her voice. "I'm afraid he may be trying to teach Timmy some of his favorite words. Who knows what his favorite jokes are like?"

Ace frowned. He studied Timmy, who had wandered into the back room, plopped down on the floor and was playing with a checkerboard. He was humming in that sweet off-key way little kids did. Blissful. Unaware of what was to come in his life.

"He needs a father," Ace said softly.

Now Crystal was the one who was frowning. "We're fine, Ace," she said. "No fathers need apply."

But she knew he wasn't applying.

"You're a good mother. I can hear it in your voice, see it when you hold him. Even in the way you take his hand and worry about him so much. I didn't mean that you, as a parent, were lacking in any way. And no, I wasn't applying for the post. I wouldn't be a suitable role model. Fatherhood isn't my style."

Her heart hurt to hear that. It was one thing to say that he didn't want to marry and settle down. It was another to declare himself unfit for fatherhood. But maybe he was right. Not every man was made to be a father. No one knew that better than she did. She supposed Ace knew a thing or two about that himself.

"We'll be fine," she promised, and she didn't know if she was promising herself or Ace or even Timmy.

"I'll be back after work."

She blinked.

He smiled and planted a soft kiss on her lips. In answer, her lips parted and he groaned, nudging closer.

She melted against him, feeling the crispness of his suit, breathing in the male scent of him, throwing all caution aside as his mouth moved over hers. She could stay here forever; she could think of nothing more she wanted to do than to make love with Ace Carson.

And then the reality of what she was doing hit her.

She placed her hands against his chest, tore her lips away, backed up. She pressed her fingers to her lips.

"I don't want to do that with you," she said firmly.

He studied her, his eyes fierce with desire and denial. Then he gave her a curt nod, shook his head and smiled. "Well, that makes one of us, because I very definitely want to do that with you. But I won't go where you don't want to go. I'll be back."

"No."

"Not for this. Just to check up on you. And to feed you."

"Why?"

He grinned then. "Why not? You have to eat, Timmy has to eat, I have to eat. And I don't think Nola Warburn is going to begin offering me meals with my room. We'll go out. My treat."

She didn't answer. She watched him walk away from her, tall and broad-shouldered and alone. She wondered how much of his life he'd spent alone.

She wondered if she really was going to have dinner with him. And whether she'd call a halt to things the next time he kissed her.

Seven

Crystal was finishing up some paperwork when her phone rang.

It was Fiona. "Almost ready for lunch?" she asked.

"Just about. Why? You looking for a companion?"

"Something like that. I thought we'd go over to Mission Creek Motors."

"Fiona," Crystal said warningly. "Just stop this right now. Ace Carson and I aren't going to be an item."

"You're not even the least bit interested in him?"

"Not a bit," she lied.

"Then you don't want to see what happens when Daddy goes to see him at the dealership?"

Crystal sucked in a breath. A vision of the pain that lurked in the depths of Ace's eyes assaulted her. He tried to hide it behind grins and tough talk, but it was clear that Ace had some unpleasant things in his history, and some of them involved Ford.

"It's not really any of my business," she said.

"Um, and Branson Hines wasn't really any of his business last night, either."

"What's *your* interest?" Crystal wanted to know.

"I think that should be obvious. The man claims

to be Daddy's long-lost son, and Dad's heart works pretty well since his surgery but he still needs to watch his diet and stress levels. I have a very definite interest. In both of them.''

"Ace wouldn't appreciate us being there."

"How do you know that? You don't even know him."

"Exactly." But she knew that this meeting wouldn't be easy for him. Of course, he'd known that when he'd decided to come here, and he'd come, anyway.

"Anybody who heard what was going on last night will be gathering around. Like buzzards waiting to see blood. We could at least do crowd control."

"You're reaching, Fiona." But Crystal couldn't help laughing.

"Maybe Ace needs a friend," her friend said softly. "And maybe I do, too, because I'm going whether you come with me or not."

Crystal thought about that. She loved Fiona, but two Mission Creek Carsons against one illegitimate Carson? The odds just didn't seem right.

"I'll meet you there," she said. "Heaven knows how this is going to look or how we're going to explain it."

Ace was helping a customer when he looked up and saw Ford Carson walk into Mission Creek Motors. Into enemy territory.

He wondered if Ford visited the competition on a regular basis, but when the man turned his way and began walking toward him, Ace had his answer. Ford was only here for one reason: To see him.

For the first time in years, Ace's palms felt sweaty.

Anger welled up in him. Ignoring Ford's advance, he turned to his elderly customer. "As you can see, this vehicle not only has all the comforts of home, Mrs. Vedemen, but it also is the exact same shade of blue as your eyes."

The white-haired lady ducked her head and chuckled. "I didn't come in here to buy a car, Mr. Carson. I came to see if you were as outrageous and flirtatious as I've been led to believe."

He smiled and shrugged. "I only speak the truth." And he realized that he had indeed been telling the truth. Louise Vedemen might be close to eighty, but she still had clear blue eyes that held a trace of mischief.

"I believe my friend was wrong about you, Mr. Carson. You're even more outrageous than I'd expected, but you know, you just might be right about my eyes and this car. I've got money and I need some fun. Why shouldn't I do something bold and silly like buying a car to complement one of the few assets I can still call my own?"

"I'm sure you have other assets," he told the woman. "A cheerful disposition, a winning smile, honesty and directness. Those count."

"Yes, they do, young man," she said, turning serious. "And looking out for your fellow man counts, too. I hear that you saved Crystal Bennett from an assault last night. That shows character."

Her words echoed around the showroom. They reminded Ace that Ford was standing not ten feet away, waiting. The man made no pretense of talking to other customers or salesmen. He simply waited, arms folded.

Ace wasn't too happy about having last night's incident reviewed in front of Ford. He hadn't come here to impress anyone. Besides, thinking of the incident at the ribbon-cutting ceremony only reminded him of what he'd felt when he saw Hines cornering Crystal the day before. The violence of his reaction surprised him even now. "I'm afraid character had little to do with it," he told his customer. "More like blind anger."

She lifted one shoulder in a gesture of dismissal. "The result was the same. You saved Crystal. Now, what do we need to do to finalize my purchase of this car?"

"Step over here," Ace said, and he led her past Ford to a large mahogany desk in the corner. A half hour later he took Mrs. Vedemen's hand in his own. "Enjoy your car," he told her. "Have fun with it."

He watched as she left the dealership. He glanced at Ford, who was standing there chatting with a customer as if he was in charge here, as well as down the street at Lone Star Auto.

He also saw that a small crowd was gathering, and that Fiona and Crystal were a part of that crowd. Ace looked at Crystal and raised a brow.

She blushed prettily and managed to look about as uncomfortable as a woman could. He'd just bet that Fiona had talked her into coming here today. He'd also bet that she was here in part because she was worried about what would happen between him and Ford. She was doing that mothering thing again, as if he needed her as much as Timmy did. She obviously felt that she owed him something for his actions last night.

A curious warmth spread through him, but he fought it down. He had no business dwelling on the worried look in her eyes or on the fact that he felt a strange desire to go to her, take her in his arms and tell her that everything would be all right.

She'd heard those kinds of lies before and she didn't need to hear them from him, a man she already knew enough not to trust too far. She was a woman who needed stability like most people needed air, and he was a man who'd spent his life fighting the outward trappings of stability. He'd chosen a wild untamed road where she didn't belong and would never feel comfortable. It was a road that would be very wrong for a woman with a child. So he had no business zeroing in on her. Besides, he needed all his wits about him to deal with the man who was waiting for him.

He turned toward Ford. As if his glance were a homing beacon, Ford also turned and looked at the man he had fathered thirty-six years ago. He walked toward Ace. When he was three feet away, he stopped.

"Looking for a car, Ford?" Ace asked.

"Looking for you."

"Why is that?"

Ford shook his head as if shaking off a pesky fly. "I just wanted to tell you... Yesterday when we talked, I didn't tell you one thing. I do remember her."

"But she was just one of your women." Ace couldn't keep the ugliness out of his voice.

Ford narrowed his eyes. "That wasn't the way of it."

"Are you going to tell me you were in love with her? That even though that was true, you got her pregnant and left her alone to face the consequences?"

"We weren't in love, no. That wasn't the way it was."

"For you. It was different for her."

Ford nodded. "Well then, I didn't know that."

"She was your housekeeper. You took advantage of that."

Silence. "I did."

Ace wanted to hit him, but this wasn't like handling Branson last night. And Ford was not a young man.

"Let me ask you one thing. Did you know she was pregnant?" Ace's voice didn't waver, though it was shot through with anger.

"Not at first."

Not at first. Which meant that he had known somewhere along the line.

"She wasn't good enough for the Carsons," Ace said as calmly as he could. "That was what your father told her when he overheard her crying to a friend on the phone about her condition. He couldn't have his son marrying her kind, not the hired help who slept around. Instead, he gave her money and sent her away without a reference. She took it because her mother was sick and needed medicine—and maybe because she knew she had already lost. You didn't stop it, any of it. Even if you didn't know what was happening, even if you didn't know she was pregnant, you must have known there was a chance she was. Especially after she left.''

A muscle twitched in Ford's jaw. "That's true. I *should* have known.''

"And when you did—finally—why didn't you go to see her?''

Ford shook his head. "No good answer to that, son. None that would satisfy you.''

But as Ace watched the man who had fathered him walk away, he knew the answer. His mother had never been good enough for Ford, just as his grandfather had said. She had been reaching above her "station,'' a term he'd heard all his life.

Arriving at the door, Ford turned and looked back. Across what seemed like the miles of showroom he spoke. "I've made mistakes in my life. Lots of them. Maybe this was the biggest.''

"And if you could change things?'' Ace asked.

Ford turned. He glanced at Fiona, then back at Ace, strain written in every line of his face. "No, I wouldn't change things. Not in the way you mean.''

And he left the building.

Fiona walked up to Ace, her eyes big and sad. "Eventually we'll have to talk. You know that,'' she said, and then she went out the door after her father.

Ace stood there as seconds ticked by, unable to move, or even to think. Finally he turned toward Crystal. There were unshed tears in her eyes. He felt a bit like crying himself, but that wouldn't help a thing. One thing he knew. He didn't want Crystal feeling sorry for him. He didn't want her to be sad at all.

So he drew on old resources. He forced a smile and walked up to her. "Looking for a car? I can offer you something with white leather seats and all the luxuries of home," he teased.

She pasted on her own smile. "You haven't seen much of the inside of my home. *Luxury* wouldn't be your word of choice. Any one of these cars probably exceeds the cost of my total worldly assets."

"Ah, so you didn't come looking for a car? Maybe a little social work? Taking care of the stranger in town?"

"I doubt that you qualify as a stranger anymore. I hear you've been flirting with all the little old ladies and that you sold Louise Vedemen a car."

"She's a nice woman."

"Yes, she is, and in spite of her money, she doesn't get enough attention. Thank you."

"Don't thank me. It wasn't as if I didn't get anything out of the deal. She bought a car."

"And if she hadn't?"

He shrugged. "She would still have been nice. Money doesn't make the woman."

"Good to know." She gave him a small smile.

"Well, we both know that I admire you greatly, even if one of these cars is worth more than your worldly assets. You do know that, don't you? I wouldn't use you for my own purposes."

She almost flinched. She supposed he was telling her that he wasn't like his father. "I've known Ford a long time," she said. "Something isn't right here. And I can see that he wants to get to know you. He wants the past to be different. Fiona already considers you a Carson."

He shook his head. "I'm not, not in the way she is, and I'm not going to be. I didn't come here to try to worm my way into the Carson family."

No, she thought. He had come here to let the Carsons know that he existed and obviously to humiliate them a little, judging by his choice of occupation and living quarters. Ford had to know that, and yet he'd come here and had this very public meeting with Ace. A meeting in which Ford had not shown particularly well. Something wasn't at all what it should be. For either Ace or Ford. Both of them appeared to be hurting.

Crystal didn't like her friends to hurt, but at least Ford had his family. All of it.

She was afraid of getting too close to Ace, but as she remembered that exchange from a few minutes ago, as she realized what it must have been like growing up without a father and then coming to the town where that same father was practically a god, she knew that she wasn't going to be able to maintain the distance she needed.

"So everything is working out here at Mission Creek Motors? If Louise is any indication, business is going well," she said casually.

He laughed then. "I'm not hurting because I've decided to take on the Carsons in a very public way, if that's what you mean," he said. "But it's going to get even better. J.D. has a good product. He just needs a little innovation, some incentive to bring people in.''

After today's scenario, Crystal thought that people might come in for a day or two just to get a look at Ace, but she knew that wasn't what he meant.

"You have ideas, I take it," she said.

"A few. This Saturday we're having the first family day at Mission Creek Motors. Strolling musicians, a display of autos through the ages, a petting zoo, food and a fireworks display at the end of the evening.''

She widened her eyes. "J.D. agreed to this?" J.D. hated to spend money.

Ace shrugged. "It'll set him back a few bucks, but it'll get people talking and coming in for a long time to come.''

"How did you organize this so fast?"

He grinned. "Some people just like to be persuaded. I did some persuading.''

That I-feel-like-I've-known-you-forever-darlin' charm of his, she was guessing. Ford should be proud of his son. She hoped he could see beyond Ace's anger. More than that, she wished there was some way to change the past and mend what appeared to be unmendable.

"Will you come?" he asked. "And bring Timmy?"

She smiled. "How could I miss it? I love petting zoos. Especially if there are rabbits. I love rabbits.''

"I'll make sure we have some.''

Crystal turned to go.

"Hey, darlin'," he said, gently catching her hand.

She looked back over her shoulder and he reeled her in slowly, in front of all the customers and salespeople in Mission Creek Motors.

"Thank you," he said.

"For what?"

He shrugged. "For being here."

She blushed. How could she tell him that she hadn't been able to stay away from him? "It was Fiona's idea," she said a bit lamely. "She practically dragged me here."

"I'm sure that's true," Ace said, "but Fiona's long gone and you're not."

She gave up any hope of pretense. "I don't even have a good reason for that."

"And I don't have a good reason for being glad. But I am." And he leaned forward and kissed her. Slowly.

Someone gave a low whistle. "Do all the female customers get one of those today?" one woman called out.

Ace raised his head. "This lady's not a customer."

But as she left the showroom, Crystal wondered, What was she to Ace? And what was he to her?

Well, she knew the answer to the second question. He was a man she shouldn't be kissing.

But if the opportunity rose again, she was pretty sure she would take it. As long as she didn't let things go any further than kissing, she would be all right. She hoped.

Family Day at Mission Creek Motors had been going just fine, but all the time Ace was welcoming people, inviting them to have some refreshments and serving as guide and baby-sitter, he was very aware that something was missing.

Crystal hadn't shown up.

An emergency? he wondered. Or maybe she was tired of playing with fire. When he'd kissed her the other day, flames had licked at him; he'd wanted to pull her closer and do wicked things to her body. If they'd been alone, he might have done just that. But he was pretty sure that Crystal wouldn't like taking things to the next level. At least not yet. She was like one of those rabbits she claimed to love—gentle but very nervous, and she had good reason to be.

Treat her gently, Carson, he warned himself. No false moves, no false promises.

He knew that this thing between him and Ford bothered her, maybe even hurt her a bit. He wanted to make it right for her, but it was one of those things that could not be made right. Things had happened in his past that could never be changed. The very thought that anyone might think he was angling for a spot in the Carson family made his hands clammy. He could never be a Carson. Would never be. But what he could and would do was prove that he was capable of being as successful as any Carson. And he would do it single-handedly. He would make his way alone, just as his mother had.

Now, looking around him at Family Day, at the smiling faces and the people who had approached J.D. about future sales, Ace could almost feel success at hand.

So why wasn't he feeling better?

He looked over the crowd, but he didn't see any women with hair the shade of sunset or eyes that made a man get lost while standing still.

"Mommy, are there bunnies?" The little voice cut through the crowd, and Ace turned to see Crystal kneeling next to Timmy by the rest-room door, struggling to tuck in his shirt as the little boy moved forward, eager to be off to the next new thing.

"I'm sure there will be bunnies, sweetie," she said. "I have it on good authority."

Ace couldn't help smiling at the picture they made. He stepped forward, holding out his hand. "Allow me to escort you directly to the bunnies, wildcat," he said. "I hear they're especially cute this morning. Just waiting for a guy like you to pet them."

"What's their names?" Timmy asked.

"Um, er…" Ace looked over into Crystal's laughing eyes. "Well, I haven't made their acquaintance yet myself."

Timmy looked worried. "For real you got bunnies?"

"Only one way to find out." Ace took Timmy's hand and slipped one arm around Crystal's waist. "Lots of people in here. Wouldn't want you to get jostled," he said.

"No, we wouldn't want that," she said, and her voice sounded slightly breathless. He loved the sound of her when she was breathless. A surge of desire hit him, a need to make her even more breathless by kissing his way down her body and then back up again. He wanted to see her, all of her, pale against the sheets in his bed. And he wanted to bring her pleasure and to share that pleasure as he braced himself above her and joined his body to hers.

The image and the ensuing sensation were too much. Way too much for such a public place. His hand tightened, and he felt her flinch. "Sorry," he said, loosening his grip. He looked down at her and saw that she was studying him carefully. He knew the minute she realized that he'd been imagining her naked in his arms, because he saw her eyes go wide and he felt the gasp climbing through her.

"Shh," he said near her ear. "We're only going to see the bunnies, remember?"

Her eyes flashed hotly at him. "They better be good bunnies," she said.

"The best," he promised. And they were.

Hours later, when the last of the fireworks had sparkled in the sky and Timmy was sleeping on the blanket where they'd placed him, Ace took Crystal's hand. "Best Family Day ever," he said.

"You've done this before?"

"Never."

She smiled. "You were so good with everyone. Helping Ms. Denny when she couldn't find her cane and asking Floyd Barger to tell you about his old model T. You knew that neither of them could afford so much as a hubcap on one of these cars." She gestured to the showroom off to their left.

"That wasn't the point. It's Family Day. It's bigger than selling cars."

She placed her hand over his. "You're a good man, Ace Carson. I hope everyone knows that."

But that wasn't why he'd come, was it? To make

people think he was a good man? If people thought that, they'd think that he was trying to win a spot in the Carson family.

Being a Mission Creek Carson was the last thing he wanted.

Well, maybe not the last thing, at least not today. The last thing he wanted to do was to hurt Crystal Bennett. But the way he was beginning to ache for her was downright dangerous. A danger aimed right at Crystal.

It had been two days since Ace had kissed her and made her forget that she was standing in an auto dealership lusting after a man she couldn't possibly have—a man who was messing with her mind. And her work, she thought, glancing down at the doodles on the page in front of her. A lopsided bunny. A convertible. A man's face. Not a good rendition of a man's face, but close enough that someone coming along might recognize the family features.

"Agh!" she said, crumpling the paper into a ball and pitching it toward the garbage can. She missed. It was past time to get her mind back on track. Someone else must have had the same idea because just at that moment her phone rang.

"Crystal?"

At the sound of Ace's voice, Crystal's body started to tingle. She glanced nervously at the crunched-up piece of paper on the floor as if he might actually see what she'd done.

"I'm here," she said, realizing she hadn't yet spoken.

"Good. I just wanted to make sure everything was all right. Make sure you recovered from your late night out Saturday and that everything else was okay. Hines is an unpredictable sort."

She couldn't help smiling. No one other than her mother had ever worried about her. Certainly her father had barely even noticed that she existed before he walked out, and John hadn't even called to see if she'd had the baby.

"I'm okay," she said. "I think maybe Branson was just drunk the other day and maybe a bit maudlin about the past. But thank you for calling anyway."

She knew she sounded prim. She didn't want Ace to think that she wanted to see him again, even though there was a part of her that ached to see him. Giving in to that ache would only end in pain. She had to think about what to do about Ace, and she would. Later.

But later she walked into her house and pressed the button on her answering machine. Loud music poured into her living room. A man's voice, distorted and thick, like a record being played at the wrong speed, came on. And what he said had her fumbling to cover her ears and to turn the machine off. But her fingers shook. She yanked the cord from the socket and slid down to the ground.

What the caller had suggested was obscene, and he'd clearly gotten more excited as the message went on.

She stilled her shaking hands against her sides. What should she do? She could call the police, but her caller ID listed the source as unknown. It could have been Branson, but it could also have been a kid making random calls and trying to make himself sound older.

She could call Ace. Ace wanted to protect her.

Right now she wanted Ace's arms around her, but that was a desire she couldn't allow herself. She had never had a man to protect her, and Ace wasn't staying. When he was gone she would be the only one to take care of herself and Timmy.

She had a son. She had to be strong, as she'd always had to be strong.

In the end she realized there was nothing she could do except hope the person didn't call back. He probably wouldn't. She'd had friends who had received obscene calls, and the caller never called back. This was only frightening because it was the first time it had ever happened to her.

Thank goodness she had taken Timmy upstairs. He had been playing in his room when she'd played back the message.

But when the phone rang again, she nearly jumped out of her shoes. She stared at the telephone as though it was an Uzi aimed at her midsection. Her hand trembled as she reached for the phone, then hesitated.

Three rings, four, five, six. The answering machine was unplugged. Eventually the person would give up. But Fiona had told her she'd call her tonight. Fiona knew she always left her answering machine on and would worry if she didn't pick up.

Carefully Crystal lifted the receiver.

"Hi, angel." Ace had never called her that before. His voice and the way he drawled the endearment filled her with warmth. One slow tear of relief coursed down her cheek.

"Two calls in one day?" she asked, forcing her voice into lightness.

"Three," he said, and she nearly dropped the receiver. "I must have just missed you leaving work the second time. Your assistant gave me your number."

She realized that he hadn't had her home number before.

"Are you calling to check up on me again?" she asked. "Not much time between the last call and this one." But something had happened. Something she didn't want him to know. If he knew, he'd come to her. And if he came here, she would give him more than she should in her present distressed state. She knew that with every ounce of her being.

He laughed. "I'm calling because I have a...well, a situation that's come up."

"A situation? Involving what?"

"Bert."

"Excuse me?"

"You know the two bunnies that Timmy wanted to call Bert and Ernie? Well, it seems that Bert is actually a Beatrice and now he's gone and had baby Berts."

She smiled. "And this would affect you how?"

He sighed. "The petting zoo called me. They knew that there had been lots of kids here on Saturday, and the bunnies were still fresh in their minds. It seems they have more than enough bunnies and they can't supply any more homes. If they can't locate homes, they'll go to a shelter and if they don't find homes there, well..."

He didn't have to go on. She knew what happened to unwanted pets.

"So you're looking for homes for bunnies?" she asked softly.

"Well, maybe a few. I've still got some calls to make, some leads I can follow, but I thought...you know, Timmy just seemed to like them so much..."

He sounded like a little boy himself.

She chuckled. "We'll take one as long as it's not a girl."

"Hmm, you like boy bunnies better than girl bunnies?" His voice was low and sensual and suggestive. If he'd been standing next to her, she would have slapped his wrist—and then she would have kissed him.

"It's only that boys have certain deficiencies that girls don't have," she said sweetly.

"Deficiencies? Oh, yes, you're right. Deficiencies," he agreed. "No future baby bunnies to worry about."

"I think one would be more than enough for a three-year-old boy to handle," she said.

"Then you'll take one?" he asked.

"Definitely."

"You're an angel. I'll bring Bert the Second over tomorrow."

"That'll be nice," she whispered.

"Crystal?"

"Hmm?"

"I'm going to hang up now, darlin', and let you

have your dinner because I know you haven't had time to eat yet. But I just have to tell you one thing.''

''What's that?''

''You have the nicest, sexiest voice of any woman I've ever known. It'll make for some seriously exciting dreams tonight.''

And as the click sounded in her ear, she couldn't help thinking that he had the nicest voice of any man she'd known. He had completely chased away the awful feeling that earlier message had given her.

She loved the sound of Ace murmuring in her ear. And tomorrow he would be coming to see her.

It would be wrong to get excited. But impossible not to.

The man was just too much for a woman like her to handle.

Eight

"**D**on't worry, little buddy, I've got you safe." Ace stood in the hospital corridor the next day whispering to the shivering little black-and-white rabbit who was backed into one corner of the carrying cage. "Soon we'll get you into bigger quarters and give you a big meal and a cushy life with the Bennetts. It's gonna be easy street for you from here on out."

"May I help you, sir?"

Ace looked up from the cage and stared into the concerned eyes of a nurse. She had her arms crossed. She didn't look like the type to talk to rabbits. If he'd been a blushing man, he would probably have done just that.

"Special delivery," he said.

She frowned. "We don't allow animals in here."

"That's too bad. Animals are like medicine to some people," he said in a low voice. He gave her a smile. "And this one's special."

"So you said."

"He's going to a home with Ms. Bennett. She and Timmy need some company. You look like a kind woman, Nurse Thompson," he said, reading her tag and hoping that he was right about her. "Make me a happy man and take me to Ms. Bennett?'' He used his best bedroom voice.

The woman gave a big hearty laugh. ''Crystal is in big trouble, I think, Mr. Carson. Oh, yes, I realize who you are now. You've got that Carson look about you. The eyes, I think, and maybe the jaw. Definitely the charm. All right, follow me, but don't even think about bringing anything bigger than that rabbit in here. Kind of cute, though, isn't he?''

''He's a ladykiller,'' Ace agreed.

Nurse Thompson practically tittered. She took him straight to Crystal's door.

''You lucky woman, you,'' she said as she left.

Crystal's brows rose. ''What did you do to her? Deirdre Thompson has ice water running in her veins most of the time.''

Ace shrugged. ''I told her that she was every man's midnight fantasy and that she'd look great in a bustier and black lace stockings.''

''You didn't!''

He grinned sheepishly. ''I didn't. But come to think of it, I do know one woman who could make a man's mouth water in a bustier and black lace stockings. Of course, you make a gray business suit look pretty sexy, too. Your tie's undone.''

''Excuse me?'' The blush that bloomed on her creamy skin was enough to make any man burst into flames. Ace couldn't help being so susceptible. Taking advantage of her confusion, he set down Bert's cage on her desk and stepped close. He gently nudged her chin up with one finger and proceeded to tie the royal-blue string tie she was wearing, the only splash of color against her white blouse and stark gray suit. His fingers lightly brushed the warm silk of her blouse where the heat of her skin came through. His fingers shook. He couldn't remember the last time he'd lost control like that when he touched a woman. Maybe never.

"There. That's better," he whispered. Although that wasn't strictly the truth. Better would have been if he had removed her tie completely, if he'd removed every other article of clothing she was wearing, as well.

"I…thank you," she whispered and took a tiny step back. He noticed that her hands were shaking, too. "I didn't realize that you were going to bring the rabbit here. I thought I'd stop by the dealership after work. Wasn't that the plan?"

He smiled. "Very definitely. That was the plan." But this one had gone awry the same way his plan to come here and thumb his nose at the Carsons seemed to be going awry. Fiona had called him again this morning. She told him that she'd been trying to reach him, but that he seemed to spend all his time at work. She said that she liked him and that she forgave him for upsetting her father. She figured there were lots of things that happened in lots of people's pasts that they regretted, and maybe her father regretted not having treated Rebecca better, but he'd had a good life and loved his wife and kids and he couldn't very well regret that, could he? Her voice had been going a mile a minute as if she was begging him to understand. He did understand, but that didn't change how much damage had been done by one man's inability to live up to his responsibilities. It didn't mend the wounds Ford's complete thoughtlessness and cruelty had caused.

"Ace?"

He looked down at Crystal, who was looking worried. Without thought, he traced one thumb down the soft skin of her jaw. He felt the pulse jump beneath his touch. "I'm sorry I changed the plans," he said, "but Bert was delivered to the dealership this afternoon and he was so nervous and jumpy and scared that J.D. was having a fit. He was afraid that Bert was, um, going to lose his breakfast in the dealership and chase all the customers away. As if something this tiny could scare anyone away. Anyway, I just thought it might be best to bring him to Timmy right away. I'm betting your son will make him feel better soon."

She smiled at that. "You act so tough, Carson. But I notice that Bert seems to be looking at you like you just gave him the biggest, juiciest carrot in the world. He likes you, and something that small and scared wouldn't like you if you hadn't treated him right. Who would have thought, that first day when you called me darlin' and commented on my legs and looked generally about as cocky as a man could look, that you'd turn out to be such a sensitive guy?"

He frowned. "Don't start talking crazy talk. I'm just here to deliver the rabbit, darlin'."

He emphasized the endearment, determined to remind her that he wasn't the kind of man a woman like her deserved. And he couldn't change. He'd been this way too long. He had to be this way, because he remembered all too well the consequences of trying too hard to fit in, of believing in dreams. He couldn't go back to that.

She studied him for long seconds, then nodded. "Let's go find my son." She emphasized the word *son,* and he knew it was a reminder to both of them that she had responsibilities and that those responsibilities ruled her life. No matter how tempted by lust either of them were, the fact remained that a child could be hurt if they made any mistakes.

"Lead on," he said, and he followed her down the hall.

"Oh, Crystal," a woman called, rushing toward them before they'd even gotten near the day-care center sign at the end of the hallway. "I was just going to come looking for you."

"What's wrong? Is Timmy okay?" Crystal asked, her voice gone trembly and high and her hands clenched into white-knuckled fists.

"He's fine. That's not what I meant. Sorry," the woman said. Ace looked at her name tag. It identified her as the director of the day-care center. "It's just that something happened while I was on my break, and I thought you'd like to know."

Crystal waited, looking like a frail blossom losing its petals in the fall winds. Ace stepped close and put his arm around her slender shoulders. She leaned against him.

"A man apparently came by while I was out," the woman said. "He said he was Timmy's uncle. The girl who met him at the door is relatively new. She doesn't know you, and she doesn't know that you don't have any brothers or sisters. Of course, it could have been someone related to John, I suppose. He *did* have a brother, I remember, and I guess he could have had one of those moments people have when they regret things they've done or haven't done in their lifetimes. I suppose that's the way it could have been."

"Did he ask to see Timmy? Did he talk to him?" Crystal asked.

"No, but he left a teddy bear for him. A huge teddy bear. It's in the day-care center now. I wasn't sure what to do. It's not a crime for someone to give a person an unsolicited gift, but this is a *child* the gift is going to and…well, running a day-care center is a touchy business at times. The ordinary rules don't always apply here."

"Do you have a description of the man?" Ace asked.

"Not much of one. Thin. Blond. Could have been anyone."

"You didn't give the bear to Timmy, did you?" Crystal asked, her shoulder tense beneath Ace's palm.

"Without asking your permission? Of course not."

Crystal gave a tight nod. "Sorry, you're right. And I'm glad that you didn't. Don't."

"Do you want to go get him and take him home?" Ace asked.

"Yes, but I probably shouldn't. It might scare him because he won't understand why he's going home early, but for today, yes, I need him to be with me. I'm going to take the next few hours off myself."

"I wouldn't worry about giving him an excuse,"

Ace said. He massaged her shoulder, wanting to give her some warmth, a sense of safety. "We've got the perfect explanation. Today is a special occasion."

Crystal frowned and shook her head. "I don't understand."

He held up the cage. "Bert. This little guy's scared. He needs Timmy, and that's no lie. We might as well let them get acquainted as soon as possible."

"Thank you," she said, and she gave him a genuine smile as she asked the director to go get her son. When the woman had gone, Crystal slumped against Ace. "Thank you again," she said, turning her face into his suit jacket.

Warmth spiraled through his body. She was so slender, so fragile, she had so much responsibility, so many worries. "You think it was Branson, don't you."

"I...I'm not sure, but after what happened at the ribbon-cutting ceremony and that phone call yesterday, I—"

"What phone call?" He pulled back from her and tucked his finger gently beneath her chin, urging her to look at him.

Big worried hazel eyes stared back. She took a deep breath. "I didn't want to tell you, but I got an obscene phone call yesterday. It was on my machine when I came home, and whoever left it tried to disguise his voice."

His hand tightened involuntarily. She flinched and he loosened up, but he didn't let go. "You had an obscene phone call on your machine when you came home, but you didn't let me know when I talked to you last night. Why?" The word came out more harshly than he'd intended. He didn't apologize.

"What could you do? I didn't even know who it was from."

His frown intensified. "Crystal, you're an intelligent woman. Last week a man threatened you and tried to assault you. This week you get an obscene phone call. You know who it is. I'm not going to let him do this to you."

"I thought it *might* be him," she said, "but I have no proof, nothing to take to the authorities, and I can't bring these things to you, Ace. *I* have to take care of my son and myself. I'm all I've got, all I've ever had."

And all I'll ever have. Ace finished the thought in his mind. That was what she meant. She wanted her independence; she needed to feel that she was in charge, in control, that she was capable of doing it all because this was the way it was going to be for her forever.

Maybe she was right.

He shook his head. "You don't have to become overly dependent on me," he said softly. "But let me help you now. Just until we can bring this information to the police and make sure that Hines is safely out of the picture. You can't always do it all yourself, Crystal. Everyone has friends who help them when times are hard."

"Do you?"

Okay, she had him. "Maybe if I didn't move around so much, I would. But even I would call on the help of a stranger if there was an emergency, lady,'' he drawled. Persuasively, he hoped.

He took a deep breath, knowing that what he was going to say next was absolutely not fair. It didn't matter. ''You have a son you're trying desperately to protect, but you have to sleep sometime. You have to let down your guard now and then.''

''Do you think I don't know that? That I haven't lived all his life realizing what would happen if anything happened to me?''

''I suppose you have. I'm sorry. I didn't make that comment to upset you, but only to suggest that if there were two of us watching him, we'd have a better chance.''

She closed her eyes, and her shoulders slumped. ''There aren't two of us. Not really.''

''There could be.''

Her eyes grew wary. She looked full into his face and took a deep breath. ''What are you saying?''

What he was saying was something she wouldn't like. At all. That wasn't going to stop him, however.

''I think I should come sleep on your couch for a few days.''

''A bodyguard?'' Her voice rose.

''Something like that.''

''You'll be in my house night and day?'' A neon sign couldn't have given off a louder hum of electricity than what passed between them at that moment.

''When I'm not at work,'' he answered, his voice thick at the thought of being in her house at night in those hours when the strongest of men and women sometimes become weak.

"You'll sleep on the couch, you said?"

"Or the floor if you prefer," he said with a lazy smile.

"I don't think this is a good idea."

"No, it's not, but I don't have a better one."

She let out a sigh. "Neither do I. And the couch will be fine," she said, sucking in her lower lip like a young nervous girl contemplating her first hours alone with a boy in the back seat of a car.

"It's settled, then," he said, smoothing back her hair where it had slipped forward over her shoulder.

"Not quite." She touched his sleeve.

He waited.

"I get a security guard," she said, "but what do you get?"

He got relief from the terror of thinking she might get caught in a madman's clutches while he wasn't there to stop it, but he couldn't say that. The truth would scare her. It scared him that he could worry so much about a woman he hardly knew.

"What do I get?" he said, pasting on a grin. "I get out of the Overton Apartments."

She smiled and crossed her arms. "I thought you liked it there."

He smiled back. "Too noisy. Nola and her customers are up all hours taking care of business, but I have to get up early in the morning. I'm a workingman, you know."

"You're much more than that, Ace," she said as her son came close and saw the bunny and his eyes lit up with joy. "I wonder if you even know all that you are."

He looked over Timmy's head. "Don't make the mistake of making me into more than I am, Crystal."

"Don't worry, Ace. You're safe. I'm not after your heart."

In another world and another lifetime, he would have replied that he didn't have a heart. For some reason he couldn't fathom, that line just didn't seem right here. And for the same reason, he felt a sharp pain pass through him right in the region where his heart should have been.

But he was sure it was a temporary pain. Soon enough it would pass. Right now it was important to get things back to normal, keep things light and flirtatious the way he always did.

"I know you're not after my heart. You're after my body," he told her.

He'd thought to shock her, to make her blush, to get things back on familiar ground.

"Could be you're right, *darlin'*," she drawled.

For the second time today he could almost have blushed. Instead, he simply let heat steal through him at the thought that tonight he and Crystal Bennett would be sharing a roof. Surely only good things could come of that.

Ace was in her tiny backyard setting up a temporary rabbit hutch while Timmy lay on his stomach talking to Bert through the mesh cage.

"How did you learn to do that?" Crystal asked, coming up behind Ace, who had made a quick trip home for his clothes and was now clad in jeans and a white shirt with the sleeves rolled up. His forearms were strong and tanned against the snowy cotton.

He glanced up from his work as she came near and offered him a cup of coffee. "My stepfather kept rabbits as a hobby. Taught me all I know."

"Including how to talk to one." She smiled as he gave her a startled look. "I couldn't help noticing that you and Bert were having a conversation earlier."

Was that a sheepish look on Ace's face? Was the man who could slay a thousand women's hearts with a sexy smile and discuss bustiers and lace stockings without a moment's hesitation looking slightly embarrassed? "Rabbits can be high-strung and nervous creatures. Talking to them helps soothe their fears just the way it soothes a human being's."

The way he soothed her whenever he spoke? Oh, this man had depths she wasn't sure she even wanted to plumb, good depths, quiet strength, and the ability to calm and reassure and protect frightened creatures of all kinds. But he had issues, too. Scary, unwavering, angry issues. And his biggest issues lay with this town and the people who lived here and the subject of marriage and family. He was a man who felt very strongly about offering promises he couldn't keep. So he kept moving.

Best not to think about that right now. There were other things to think about. Frightened rabbits and the safety of her son. And now another facet thrown in. If they were going to adopt the rabbit, it would become a family member. Timmy held tightly to things; he loved hard. If they took this rabbit—and it ap-

peared there was no turning back now—they must not
let it get sick or lose it.

"Will that hold him?" she asked, nodding to the
pen.

"For tonight. I'll build something more permanent
when there's time, but for now this will do. My stepfather taught me well," he said reassuringly.

"Was he a good man, then?"

Ace opened the rabbit cage and gently removed
Bert, releasing him into his new home. "He'll want
to sniff around and get used to things," he told
Timmy. "But if you talk softly to him like you've
been doing, it will help him."

Timmy looked up at Ace with adoring eyes as he
settled in front of the hutch.

Ace turned to Crystal as they moved back toward
the house. "My stepfather was the best man I ever
knew, a principal in the private school where my
mother worked in the cafeteria," he said. "He loved
her and he worked hard to make her feel like a queen,
even though she insisted on maintaining her job. It
was a rotten job, but I don't think she ever felt completely secure after what Ford's father did to her. My
stepfather loved her unconditionally, but she'd been
fighting prejudice and poverty for so long that by the
time he came along it was something she couldn't
shake."

"Prejudice because she had an illegitimate child?"
she asked softly.

"Yes, and because we were poor. The money that
Ford's father gave her was enough to cover her

mother's medicine in her last days and a little of her hospital costs when I was born, but not much more.''

Crystal frowned at that. "That doesn't seem right."

He shrugged. "None of it seemed right, but she was just a housekeeper, a nobody, a girl who'd made a foolish mistake in falling for a rich Carson, a man above her station, and Ford's father promised her that if she stayed, he'd make sure that she and her baby were shunned. He was a Carson. She knew that he could do it. As it was, things weren't much different working for Newton Academy. I was allowed to go there only because my mother worked there, but...well, let's just say we never exactly fit in."

"The kids at the school didn't accept you?"

He shrugged. "I was an interloper, a pretender, someone who didn't belong and was only there on charity. They never let me forget that."

His jaw was tight, and she knew that there was a world of meaning in his last statement. The sudden smile that didn't reach his eyes told her that he wasn't about to go into details, either, but she could just imagine that he'd learned how to fight protecting his mother's good name and defending his right to attend classes at a rich kid's school. Those skills he'd used against Branson had been honed young.

"But you had a stepfather who loved you, didn't you?"

He nodded. "Yes, I did, and I thank the heavens for that. While he was with us before he died, he tried very hard to make every day of my mother's life and mine a blessing. We were lucky he found us. I don't think I'll ever meet another man in the world I admire that much.''

And yet, she couldn't help thinking, there was a man across town he was related to. Several men, in fact. Men she'd always thought of as admirable even though she'd known they were very human. They made mistakes.

She wished the barriers between Ace and the other Carsons weren't so high. He was a good man, and he deserved to have a loving family.

Surely there was some way for him and for them.

But when she turned and saw the way Ace was looking at her, she pushed the thought from her mind.

''I didn't mean to tell you all that, and don't go getting that look in your eyes,'' he warned.

''What look?''

''That woman look, that I-want-to-fix-the-world-and-make-everyone-happy look. I'm content with my life and my ways, Crystal. Leave it alone.''

For a moment the wheels of her mind spun. Was she so transparent? Apparently. And obviously she was predictable, too, and she didn't like that one little bit. She didn't like the fact that she had upset him, either, and the only cure for that was to take his mind off the topic at hand.

''Well, I'm not happy,'' she said. ''Not at all.''

He blinked wide and his mouth fell open. She should try this unpredictable stuff more often. Aim to be mysterious and quirky.

''You're not happy? Why is that?'' His voice was dangerously low. She could tell that he was prepared to go out and slay dragons, to fix things the way he had accused her of trying to fix things. The irony made her smile.

"I'm hungry. We haven't eaten yet, you know." She grinned.

He smiled back. "All right, I'm going to report your obscene phone call and the incident at the day-care center to the police. Then we'll eat," he said, his voice dropping low on the last sentence. His words had sounded strangely like *All right, then we'll make love,* she couldn't help thinking.

"I'll just go make something," she said, turning to flee, but he caught her gently by the arm.

"I've invaded your house. I don't expect you to slave for me," he said.

"It's just cooking."

"I'll take you out."

"We can't eat out every night. It's expensive."

"Crystal."

"What?"

"I can afford it."

"It just doesn't feel right, having you pay for me and Timmy to eat."

"It's nothing. It's just money," he said.

"I can take care of us," she insisted.

"You must be hell on dates," he muttered. "I'll bet you insist on paying."

She almost gasped. "I don't."

"Well, then."

"This isn't a date."

"Pretend it is. Pretend that I'm the last guy you went out with. I take you and Timmy to a restaurant and I pay."

"I'd rather not pretend that you were the last guy I dated."

He raised a brow. "You want to clarify that?"

She shrugged. "Not much to tell. He tried to stick his hand up my dress and his tongue down my throat at the restaurant, and I went home before I'd even eaten."

Ace's countenance darkened. He swore beneath his breath. "Lady, you can do better than that. No wonder Fiona is trying to fix you up with every man who comes down the pike. Any man has got to be an improvement."

She felt a small trace of indignation. "I've had worse."

He raised one brow and smiled. "I don't intend to be worse."

She couldn't help but smile back. "I'm not a charity case, Ace."

"Lady, you are the farthest thing from a charity case that I've ever seen, but I have to agree with my half sister when she says that you need some serious courting."

"You and I are not going to get serious," she reminded him.

"No, we're not, but we're going to have some fun together while I'm here. Might as well, since I'm going to be making my home on your couch. And you can get a decent meal or two out of the deal," he coaxed. "Come on, Timmy will like it."

She rolled her eyes. "You know my soft spots."

"Not entirely as of yet, ma'am, but I'm hoping to

learn what they are,'' he said with a mock leer. And then he kissed her full on the mouth.

No question about it, she needed to stay on her toes around Ace Carson. He was a charmer, and she had a feeling she was about to be completely charmed.

Nine

Less than an hour later, Ace closed the door on the police officer who got into his squad car and drove away. He knew he looked like thunder, but he couldn't control himself. He knew that any ranting and raving was the last thing Crystal needed to hear right now, so he took a minute to pull himself together. When he turned back toward her, she was looking at him a bit anxiously, as if *she* wanted to help *him,* when it was supposed to be the other way around.

"Well," she said, "I'm no worse off than I was before, you know. They've said that they've tried to contact Branson for questioning about the incidents, but he seems to have disappeared. Beyond that, they can't just go looking for suspects on what little we've given them. I didn't really expect more than that."

He supposed he hadn't, either, but he had at least hoped to be able to offer her some reassurance, some sense that she had more protection for Timmy and herself than just him.

"You're too easygoing," he said.

"I'm not."

He chuckled at her insistence. "You are, and you're not fooling anyone by pretending otherwise."

She crossed her arms, then leaned forward until she would have been nose to nose with him if she'd been taller.

"I'm not a pushover. I know what I want and I go after it."

"Really?" He arched a brow. "Well, what do you want, darlin'?"

She lifted her chin defiantly and frowned. He could almost hear the wheels spinning as she struggled to think of a good answer. "I guess I want…food. You promised Timmy and me food, or are you reneging on the deal?"

Ace grinned. "I deliver what I promise. Always." Easy enough to do when he seldom promised anything.

Crystal leaned back and gazed at him with trusting eyes. "I believe you," she said solemnly.

That simple. That easy. She believed him even though she didn't know him.

"Come on," he said, taking her arm and moving her along, his voice a low growl. "First we feed you and then we teach you something about trusting men too easily."

"I already know about that," she whispered. And yes, he supposed she did. She didn't need someone like him giving her lessons.

At the family restaurant forty-five minutes later, Timmy's eyes were like bright moons. After they'd eaten, the waitress had brought him crayons and a sheet to color and make into a hat if you punched it out and folded it the right way. He was scribbling madly.

"What's that?" Ace asked, pointing to an indistinguishable blob.

"Bert."

"And that?" Crystal asked, gesturing to a sort of egg-shaped thing with sticks coming out of it.

"Ace."

"Um, a very good likeness," Crystal said.

Timmy looked up at her and beamed. He turned to Ace, and Ace knew he was supposed to say something appropriate.

"No one's ever made a finer picture of me, wild-cat."

Timmy sighed with contentment. He picked up a stray French fry and accidentally dropped it on his picture. The look of horror and woe that transformed his smile was immediate. His lower lip began to quiver. He turned desperate eyes to his mother.

"It's okay, honey," she said. "Everybody has accidents."

Ace knew that it wasn't okay for Timmy by the lost look on his face. Maybe it wasn't the worst thing in the world, but heck, the little boy had had some bad luck in his life, not the least of which was a father who didn't want him. Someday he'd learn about that, and it would haunt him. And today he'd been yanked out of day care and away from his buddies early. Ace was not going to let anything spoil Timmy's party mood tonight.

"An accident? You did that on purpose, didn't you, wildcat? I saw this thing on TV the other night where the artist paints with food. You must have seen it too."

Timmy looked a bit confused and taken aback. But then he looked down at the French-fry stain. He smiled and reached for the ketchup.

Crystal caught his wrist in a gentle grip. She gave Ace an exasperated-mom look. "No painting with food," she told them both. "This is a restaurant."

Timmy frowned. Ace sighed. "Shoot," he told Timmy. "I guess she's right. If we started painting with food, then everyone else here would want to do it, too, and then ours wouldn't be so special. As it is, you got in one good French-fry mark to make yours stand out. I guess we'd better be happy with that. Looks great as it is, anyway."

Timmy studied his work. He nodded slowly. "I made it. By myself." And then he smiled shyly at Ace.

"You sure did, pal. Let's take it home now." Timmy clutched his French-fry-smeared paper hat close to him as they exited the restaurant.

At home, Crystal put her son to bed. She came out with an armful of blankets. "That was pretty quick thinking back in the restaurant. Where did you learn how to handle boys on the verge of tears?"

She was looking so lovely in pale gold with the moonlight streaming in through the windows, catching the red lights in her hair. Her eyes were filled with wonder and gratitude, as if she thought he held some special key to her son's soul. He had to be honest.

"I don't know beans about handling boys, but I've walked away from my share of women. I always try to leave them happy."

She should have flinched when he said that. Maybe she should have simply turned and walked away.

Instead, she smiled slightly, a slow sad smile. "I wonder if you said that for my benefit or for yours."

"It's the truth." And it was.

"I believe you, and I guess I should be offended, but…it's nice to hear the truth, even if it isn't exactly a nice truth."

Of course. She'd heard nothing but lies from men. Now she was willing to settle for unfortunate truths.

He couldn't help himself then. He moved toward her with no thought to making her happy, only comforting her. He had to comfort her. He wanted to make her forget the lies that other man had offered her. Taking the blankets from her arms, he slipped his hands to her waist and pulled her in slowly until her body barely touched his.

"You always deserve the truth, always the truth," he whispered. And he took her mouth with his. Slowly. Very slowly. He pulled her closer.

And she came to him. She didn't resist. She was soft in his arms, warm against his heart.

He pulled back then, looking down into her eyes.

She smiled. "That was very nice. You must have made a lot of women happy."

And just like that, he felt like the jerk he was.

"Not so many," he confessed. "Definitely no women like you."

Crystal frowned in confusion. "What makes me different?"

He played with a soft strand of her hair. "You're

apple pie and ice cream, Sunday picnics, walks in the woods holding hands. Very…''

''Ordinary?''

''Special.''

''Hmm, that sounds like a lie.''

He shook his head slowly. ''Believe me, it's not.''

''But you don't do apple pie and ice cream and Sunday picnics?''

''Not usually.''

''Why?''

''Those kinds of women are too open. They get hurt by men like me.''

''So you don't want to hurt me?''

Again he shook his head. ''Definitely not.''

''But you liked kissing me?'' She seemed uncertain.

He grinned. ''Most definitely. I loved kissing you.''

''I liked kissing you, too.'' And she surprised him by sliding her hands up his chest, rising on her toes and pressing her lips to his again.

For five seconds his senses simply exploded. Sweet sensation, her softness, the honeysuckle scent of her, her mouth beneath his, all drove him insane and had him groaning. Then he caught her, slid his hand beneath her hair and deepened the kiss.

Instantly his body reacted. He was aware of every inch of her pressed against him, how small she was, how delicate, how absolutely enticing.

He slid his hands down her sides, tested the curve of her waist, the flare of her hips, the way her skin felt beneath his fingertips.

''Ace.'' She whispered into his mouth.

"Mmm?"

"Don't stop kissing me. Just because of the apple-pie thing."

He pulled back. "Not if the whole town of Mission Creek marched in here right now and demanded that I cease and desist."

Then he kissed her again slowly, savoring the flavor that was distinctly Crystal. His lips still on hers, he slid his fingers beneath the top button of her blouse. His fingers stroked lower, outlining the swell of her breast as he deftly slipped open two more buttons and slid his fingers against the lacy edges of her bra.

"Let me look at you," he whispered against her lips as he bent and kissed the curve of her breast. Gently, reverently. Her pale firm flesh drove him wild and he freed the rest of the buttons and flicked open the catch on her bra, exposing her beautiful rose-tipped breasts to his view.

Glancing up, he saw desire mixed with fear in her eyes.

"I won't hurt you," he promised, and he swore that he wouldn't.

"I believe you."

And then he slid down her, knelt before her, drawing her down to her knees, too. He bent, took the tip of one breast into his mouth.

A shudder went through her as she trembled in his arms.

He held her closer and kissed her again, only his shirt shielding her skin from his.

From another part of the small house came a clinking sound, then water running.

Crystal gasped. She fumbled with her bra. "Timmy. He gets up now and then for water."

"Shh, sunshine," Ace said, ignoring the deep throbbing of his body as he quickly fastened the clasp she couldn't seem to manage. He took two deep breaths and slowly buttoned every button. "It's okay," he said. "Do you need to go help him?" He could still feel her heart thudding against his fingers.

She shook her head. "No, he has his own special cup he likes to use. He wants to do it himself." But she looked distraught.

He caught her chin in his hand. "It wasn't your fault," he said. "I started this."

Crystal frowned. "Now who's lying? I definitely kissed you back and I asked you not to stop."

"You're a woman, Crystal. You're human."

"I'm a mother first."

He smiled. "And you're a damn good one. Just don't be too hard on yourself for this, all right? You may have kissed me, but I kissed you first. And I was the one who went beyond kissing. You didn't ask for that."

"I didn't stop it. I enjoyed it."

Oh, he wished she hadn't said that, because he was just beginning to get his desire back under control. Now the fires were flaring again.

"I'll take the blankets and set up on the couch," he said. "Let's just put tonight down to stress and nerves and the demands of the past few days."

She thought about that. "Yes, you're probably

right. That's all it is. I certainly don't go around acting like this normally.'' Her voice was strained, uncertain. She moved away and left the room, clicking the door closed behind her.

He waited until she had gone and then he sank onto the couch. He could still feel her on his fingertips, taste her on his lips. The ache to have her and complete what they'd started went deep. It made him restless.

She said she didn't go around acting like this normally. He should feel good about that. She didn't go to pieces in every man's arms. She had been saving up her passion.

For whom? Him? A man who had a bad history with the Carsons, her friends and the most prominent members of this town? He couldn't escape that, couldn't forget that past. It had colored his whole life and had changed his mother's life forever. He didn't want to be a part of this community or a part of the world Crystal inhabited. He couldn't spend his life trying to meet the requirements. He'd tried to do that when he was a boy. Tried and failed. No, he definitely could never be an apple-pie-and-ice-cream kind of man, which was what she really needed.

The passion between them was real and undeniable, but it wasn't what she needed at all.

He should keep his distance. For tonight at least he could do that. He could stay right here on this couch. And he would.

Hours later, tossing and turning on the too-small couch, Ace reiterated his intention. He would stay here on this couch, away from Crystal.

But damn, it wasn't going to be easy. The night was proving long and restless.

And who knew how he would get through tomorrow or the next few days?

One thing he knew. If she needed apple pie and ice cream then, for the next few days while he was here, he would give her that. At least that much. He'd do it because he didn't want her worrying that he'd invade her bed and then leave her alone again afterward.

For the next few days he would be the perfect gentleman.

No touching Crystal.

Deep in his soul, he howled an objection.

"Tough, buddy. Get used to celibacy. She's not yours to take." And he turned his back on his objections, wrapped the blanket around him and rolled over.

In the night he dreamed of Crystal wrapped up in the blanket with him. No surprise that she was naked.

Some things, like dreams, a man just couldn't control.

"What is that?" Crystal asked the next evening when Ace pulled up in a luxury van and wrestled a huge box out onto the ground.

"Nothing much."

She crossed her arms. "That's not much of an answer."

He flashed her a smile. "I just thought it might be nice for Timmy to get out and have some fun, so I thought maybe a drive-in. My mom and my stepdad used to do that now and then. Timmy's a little young. So I thought maybe the drive-in could come to him." He pulled out his keys and slit the box, sliding out a big-screen TV.

"Ace." That one word sounded like a warning.

"He'll like it," he said, and he almost sounded like Timmy pleading for a favor. She almost laughed at the look on his face.

"He'll get used to things like this and then when you've gone it'll be a punishment for him to return to his old life."

"No, he won't. I'll explain that this is a one-shot thing."

"Ace, please."

"I brought popcorn and a VCR and kid movies. Animated stuff. We can hook the machine up outside and sit out under the stars and pretend that we're at the drive-in."

She lowered her lashes, then looked up again. "That sounds dangerous." A slight blush warmed her cheeks and she reached up to cover them. She couldn't help thinking about what it would be like to go to a real drive-in with Ace, to be closed up in a dark car together.

She looked up at Ace and found him watching her. His eyes were narrowed and dark, like a man on the verge of taking a woman into his arms and kissing his way down her naked body.

Heat swirled through her. "Ace?" she asked, and she hated the way her voice quavered.

He stared at her fiercely for several long seconds. Then he cleared his throat.

"Under the right circumstances, it could be dangerous, but not tonight. We'll have Timmy with us. Right between us. All the time," he said. "Come on, Crystal. Say yes."

She couldn't help laughing then. "Ace, why are you doing this?"

He got a stubborn look in those gorgeous blue eyes of his. "You don't have enough fun in your lives. You mostly have men like me pawing at you or at least wishing they could. You need more fun, and so does Timmy. It was supposed to be fun. Apple-pie fun," he said simply.

Fun. He wanted her and Timmy to have a little fun in their lives. Crystal's throat nearly closed up.

"All right, thank you," she managed to say. "Thank you, yes."

So Ace set up the TV and the tape player and the couch on the lawn. Timmy hovered near, giggling and hopping up and down on one foot and generally getting in Ace's way, though the man never would say so, Crystal thought as she made dinner.

He wanted her to have fun while he was here. Before he left, he wanted to give her and her son something he thought was missing from their lives.

She knew where he was coming from, because she wanted him to have something that was missing from his life, too.

But the one thing that she kept thinking of, she knew he wouldn't like. The one thing Ace was missing was family.

What was she going to do about that?

* * *

Two days later Ace pulled onto Crystal's street after work and just sat there. For the past two days he'd been vigilant about keeping watch on her house. He'd grilled the director down at the day-care center to see if she knew anything more about the man who had delivered the teddy bear for Timmy. He'd once or twice had a feeling that he wasn't the only one watching the house, but then he was beginning to be suspicious about everyone where Crystal and Timmy were concerned. A woman alone with a little boy was vulnerable in so many ways. He wanted to wrap her up in the blanket on his couch and protect her. He wanted to warn every man on the street that she was not to be tampered with or bothered or to be taken lightly, but of course all of that was meaningless. Once he was gone, he couldn't protect her.

Ace blew out a breath, shook his head and moved his car down the street, intending to turn into the drive.

There was a car already there. Several in front of the house, too. Nice cars. Cars with the Lone Star Auto emblem on the back.

Swearing under his breath, Ace advanced on the house. "Crystal," he called.

She appeared in the door almost instantaneously. Was that an anxious look on her face? No, he must have been mistaken. She was smiling sweetly.

"Ace, I've almost got dinner ready. Come in and sit down. I…I've got a few guests over tonight. You remember Fiona and her husband, Clay, of course."

Ace turned and stared at Fiona. She smiled and waggled her fingers at him. "Hi, Ace."

He blinked. Clay coughed and rubbed one hand over his jaw. "She has no shame," he said as Fiona swatted at him. But Clay was already rising and extending his hand.

Ace took it automatically.

"And here are Cara and Omar, Matt and Rose, Josie and Flynt, too."

It was almost a complete Carson party. "Where's Ford and Grace?" he couldn't help asking.

Crystal blinked. "Well, I just thought… You're right. Of course I should have asked them. Do you think it's too late, Fiona?"

Ace placed a hand on her arm to stop her. He looked down at her, trying not to look angry. She was already looking about as nervous as a woman could look. "It wouldn't be polite to ask someone now," he said, forcing the words through his teeth. Of course, she knew he didn't want to share a table with his esteemed father, but then he didn't want to share a table with the rest of the Carsons, either, yet here they were. Children of privilege. They were the ones who would have been paying customers at the school where he had grown up. They would have been the ones who steered clear of the kitchen help's son, as if they were afraid some of the dirt of his birth would rub off on them.

"All right, Ace," she said, looking down at where his hand lay on her arm. Her warmth was like sun-kissed nectar. It drew him. He felt connected to her in some strange, sweet and yet alarmingly compelling way. She was, in fact, the only person in the room he felt any connection to. He almost didn't want to let her go, he almost *couldn't* let her go, and because he realized that, he backed away.

"I'll just go wash up," he said.

When he returned, everyone in the room was milling around, some even shuffling their feet.

"Ace, you sit here. You're the oldest son," Crystal said firmly, directing him to a chair at the head of the table.

The breath nearly slid right out of his body. He waited for someone to make an objection or at least to look away. No one did, although no one exactly looked comfortable, either.

Slowly Crystal got everyone seated. She sat down and asked Ace to say grace. Warmth suffused his face. It wasn't as if he'd never done it. His mother and stepfather had included him at home. But this wasn't home and these people weren't his family.

He raised his gaze to Crystal, who was seated beside him. Her eyes were luminous, pleading, filled with a need for something, like a child who plans a party and is anxious for everything to go right.

She moved her hand over to his and grasped it. On his other side Fiona did the same. He felt as if his chest was being crushed, as if his throat wouldn't operate. Afraid his feelings would show in his eyes, he bowed his head.

"Father, for what we are about to receive, make us truly thankful. Amen."

It was all he could get out, that rote bit of prayer, that quick call for help and praise. It was enough, however. Fiona let go of his hand. Crystal squeezed his hand before releasing it.

"So, I hear you and Dad had quite a meeting the other day," Matt said. His voice was the voice of a man used to commanding.

"I wouldn't exactly call it that," Ace said. He didn't like his father, but he didn't gossip about any man in public. Not that Matt could be judged for asking. Ford was his father, after all. He had a right to challenge the man who had challenged him.

"Fiona was there, I guess. Daddy told the rest of us something about it," Cara answered. "Of course, Mama already knew. He didn't know that your mother was pregnant, but I think you were right that day in the dealership. He could have guessed that she could be, and I'm sure he knows that. I think it's weighed on his mind a long time. Of course he knows that doesn't change anything. Not the past. Not how you feel about him."

"He ask you to say that?"

"Of course not. And he didn't tell me all that much. Just what he thought I had a right to know. That yes, you are his son, and yes, he behaved badly toward your mother and you. That's all."

Her voice was woeful, and Ace could tell that she wanted to find some way to build a bridge, to mend the old wounds. But the fact remained that Ford had eventually known that he had a child and had done nothing about it. Nothing could bridge that gap. And sitting before him were the offspring Ford had favored, the ones who had grown up having a real place in the world, whose mother had been given respect, not sneers and slurs and poverty.

"We have to start somewhere, Ace," Fiona said gently.

He looked her in the eye. "I don't see why."

"Maybe because you came here and we found out the truth," Flynt said. "If you hadn't, we could have gone on for the rest of our lives ignoring you, but now that you're here, we can't do that. You're blood. You're a Carson."

"And Carsons take care of their obligations?" he asked, raising a brow.

If another man had asked him that using the same tone of voice, he might have slugged him. Flynt looked as if he wanted to. Crystal was halfway out of her seat. The little peacemaker, Ace thought, warmth spreading through him at the thought. He squeezed her hand gently to stop her from stepping in.

Flynt stared him down. "They do," he said curtly, drawing a smile from Ace.

"Well, rest easy, then, little brother, I release you from your obligation."

"We don't want to be released," Cara said. "We want you out of the Overton Apartments."

Ace couldn't help smiling at that. "It doesn't look good to have a relative living there, does it?"

Fiona shook her head. "You know that's not what she meant, big brother."

Did he? These were Mission Creek Carsons he was talking about. Proud people who had never had that pride damaged. Being associated with Nola Warburn probably didn't sit quite right.

"Ace, give them a chance," Crystal said softly.

He turned and looked at her as she watched him

with those luminous, hopeful eyes. How could she be so hopeful of hearing good things from a man like him when she'd gotten only bad things from men before? He wanted to give her what she wanted, but tension was rising in him, cold and hard and suffocating. He knew that feeling. He tried to back away from it.

"He doesn't want to be a part of us," Matt said, studying his half brother carefully. "Isn't that true?"

"I really don't see the point," he finally said. "I'm not staying. Why bother getting to know each other?"

He could almost feel the distress radiating off Crystal. He hated himself for hurting her this way, for throwing away the gift she'd tried to give him—he knew that was what she'd been trying to do—but he just couldn't play his part here. He couldn't become the one thing he'd always tried not to be, the thing he'd always loathed.

A silence settled over the room, marred only by the clinking of silverware and the sound of Timmy playing in the next room.

"We'd better get going," Flynt offered. "Work tomorrow. Thanks for inviting us, Crystal," he said, bending to kiss her cheek. "Too bad it didn't work."

"Don't blame yourself," Matt said, taking her hand and hugging her. He stared over Crystal's fragile shoulders and gave Ace a hard look.

Ace felt like a heel. His little brother was right. He could feel Crystal questioning her motives already.

He stood and turned to her. "I appreciate what you did," he said, feeling awkward for the first time in front of her. He didn't like humbling himself in front of the Carsons, but it just wouldn't be right to leave this until they were gone. Then his words would be meaningless for her. "I do. Thank you," he said. And he nodded to the group that was hovering around Crystal as he turned to leave the room.

"You tried," Cara said to Crystal.

"The man is a stubborn mule," Fiona said loudly enough to be heard as he made it into the living room.

Ace grinned to himself, but he didn't turn around. No need to. He *was* a stubborn mule.

The sound of feet shuffling, murmured goodbyes and doors slamming filtered into the living room. He had sat down on the couch and was pretending to read the paper.

Soon he heard the front door close. The Carsons had left. Soft footsteps came closer.

He turned. She was looking so sad, shaking her head.

"They want to get to know you, Ace," she said. "Why won't you let them?"

He knew she couldn't understand, but she deserved at least some kind of explanation.

"I'm a jerk," he assured her.

"You're not."

"Any other man would have taken your gift and responded to it."

"So why didn't you? And don't tell me it's because you're a jerk."

He rose to his feet, crossed to her. She had pulled her hair back in a loose ponytail with a silver clip. It would be easy to ignore her question and just focus on her and on this physical thing that threatened to envelop him whenever she was around.

"I've spent all my life being pegged as a wanna-be," he said, sighing. "Just like at the academy, and you know about that."

"Kids are cruel," she whispered.

"But they were right, in a way. I really didn't belong there. I *was* only there because my mother was willing to demean herself cooking for selfish rich kids to give me an education. And I never deserved all her hard work. I resented my situation. I got into fights, got suspended, even spent a night in jail when I was older. I must have broken her heart a thousand times. They labeled me bright but unmotivated. What I was, however, was angry. I guess I still am."

"But you told me that your stepfather..." She halted, confused.

"Was a good man? He was. A wonderful man, in fact. But Derek didn't come on the scene until I was already in high school. For some reason he looked past my anger. He shared with me, taught me about cars and told me that I had redeeming qualities, that I had a little blarney in me and would probably be a good salesperson if I could just learn to show my better side. But Derek was only with us four years. He died not long after I graduated. After that I sold cars and other things here and there and stayed around to take care of my mother. I didn't want her taking care of rich people anymore. Three months ago, she died."

"And she told you about Ford and you came here

to make him feel a little of the humiliation your mother felt?''

"Something like that."

"And then what?"

"Then I go. I'll be free of the whole Carson thing at last and forever. I can't stay, Crystal. I'm not a Carson, even if that's my name. I wasn't born to it. I don't want it to seem like I came here looking for a handout or acceptance.''

"That wasn't what I intended."

"I know. You wanted me to have something finer, but that's not for me. I've spent a lot of my life alone. By choice. It's what works for me."

"Ace, that's not right." There was such sadness in her voice, he knew she was going to try again.

"Give up on me, Crystal." He slid his hand beneath her ponytail and cupped the curve of her neck. He leaned over and kissed her forehead. "It just won't work. You can't change things and make them right for me. And I'm fine as I am. I have all that I need.''

But as he moved from her, he knew that wasn't quite right. He was beginning to need her, need the way she made him feel, the way she made him think of someone other than himself.

Still, he couldn't use her. She was too precious, and she had that little boy. He wouldn't sacrifice either of them to the greed that lived inside him, the longings that had always gone unfulfilled. If he did, he'd be no better than the man who'd started it all.

"We'd both better get some sleep," he said, then turned to move to the living room and his couch.

"Ace?"

He turned back. She caught him by the front of his shirt, pulled him down and placed her sweet lips on his.

He forced himself not to touch her, though the taste of her, the gentle butterfly movements of her mouth were making him crazy.

Finally it was either go insane or kiss her back. He wrapped his arms around her, bent her backward over his arm and drank deeply of her lips. One kiss. Two. Ten. He couldn't get enough from her, but he tried. And then when there wasn't enough breath left between them to sustain a bird, he set her back on her feet.

She stared up at him, her chest heaving, her hair tumbling over her shoulders in a soft tangle. "Your problem isn't that you're a wanna-be, Ace. It's that you have too darn much pride."

He blinked. "So you kissed me because you're angry with me for having too much pride?"

She leaned in closer and rested her hands lightly on his chest. She gave him a listen-to-me-you-idiot-man look. "I kissed you because you make me crazy."

And with that she turned to leave the room. Just before she walked out, she looked back over her shoulder. "And because I really, really wanted to. For the record, I knew both your brothers before they were married. They were handsome, very charming and very rich men, but I never wanted to kiss either of them."

And she closed the door behind her with a click.

Need spiraled high in Ace, but he let her go. He forced himself to sit down on the couch. So she hadn't liked his half brothers well enough to be attracted to them? Interesting.

"Interesting, but not really relevant," he whispered to himself. "She still wants you to reconcile with them. You still have to leave. So just ignore what the lady said."

Like hell he would. He wanted to drive her crazy some more.

And drive himself crazy in the process.

The next time she kissed him, they would take it to the next level. At least he hoped so. He wanted to gaze down into those hazel eyes as he touched her. No woman had ever made him want that.

It was a new experience, but then, this entire trip and everything Crystal Bennett represented was a new experience for him. Might as well learn something new while he was still here.

Ten

Maybe Ace didn't have to stay here on her couch anymore, Crystal thought the next day. He couldn't be comfortable, what with his feet hanging off the end and her trying to push him into relationships with his family he clearly didn't want. She wasn't even going to think about the kissing part. Not that she thought Ace minded that part. He was very good at kissing, and he seemed to like kissing her. But then, she was pretty sure he had liked kissing any number of women in his life. She was just the one he was kissing now.

"Remember that," she said to herself. "Do not forget it."

"Remember what?"

Crystal gasped and whirled around in her chair to find Fiona standing there. "I don't know. I don't remember. You startled it out of my mind." Which was a complete lie, but she couldn't help it. She would not discuss her feelings for Ace with his half sister, a woman who was having her own struggles with Ace.

Fiona looked at her strangely, but then she shrugged. "Come on, come with me."

Crystal shook her head and smiled. "You Carsons are bossy."

"You knew that when you became my friend. You're just mad because you can't boss Ace around and make him like all of us."

"Doesn't it bother you?"

"I haven't decided yet. We're still circling each other. It's a strange relationship, Crystal."

No question about that. "Where do you want to go?"

Fiona perched on her desk. "Clay's working tonight. Let's take Timmy over to see Grace. She's been dying to spend some time with him, and then we'll go do girl stuff. Fun stuff. You could use a night out, and heaven knows I could."

"I don't know. Timmy—"

Fiona knew about the teddy-bear thing. "Timmy couldn't be any safer with Grace than if you hired fifty secret-service agents. My father has good help and good security."

That was true enough.

"I'm still not sure. Ace has been...helping me at my house."

Fiona chuckled. "Ace has been staying at your house. He's the official watchdog. That means he watches for intruders and he probably watches himself, too, for the most part."

"For the most part." Crystal gasped. "How do you know so much?"

"I'm a Carson. I have ways." She smiled slyly at Crystal. "Don't worry, we'll go check in with Ace, too. Any more objections?"

Just one. She wouldn't be with Ace tonight. The thought drifted in, along with a hefty dose of regret. It frightened her, the fact that she would start turning down time with friends in order to just look at the man, talk to the man, when there was clearly no way this could work. With Ace, it wouldn't be a matter of a man telling her he loved her, getting her pregnant and walking away. He wouldn't tell her he loved her, he wouldn't get her pregnant, but he would most definitely walk away.

That thought assaulted her. She couldn't get around it, couldn't escape it, so she took a deep breath and aimed to do the right thing. "All right, I'll go with you. Give me a second."

Within a very short while she had delivered a happy Timmy into Grace's arms, and she and Fiona were driving down the highway en route to talk to Ace.

"We could have just called," she said.

"And miss the chance to see what new event is going on over at Mission Creek Motors? Maybe it's old-movie night, or ballroom-dancing night. Do you believe that Ace had people dancing around all the cars?"

"I heard. He's been very good for Mission Creek Motors, hasn't he?"

"Better than very good, I'd say. Daddy's place looks like a tomb in comparison."

Crystal felt a trace of sadness. "Has that upset him?"

Fiona shrugged. "Can't tell. He's not talking. Here we are."

She parked and got out of the car, motioning for Crystal to follow her. But Crystal didn't need a signal. She could see Ace through the wide, plate-glass windows. He was smiling and talking to a customer, clearly enjoying himself. The customer, an elderly man, seemed to be having a good time, too. Crystal and Fiona pushed through the doors.

"So you think I'm not too old for red?" the white-haired man was saying.

"Do you feel too old for red?"

The man chuckled. "I feel like I'm twenty."

"Well, then, why don't you take her for a spin? I'll get Bill to move it out of here."

"Oh, I don't know."

"You don't have to know. There's no charge for trying it, and why deny yourself a little fun? Go cruise the main drag and check out the women."

"I'm married," the man protested.

"Well, then, give her a treat. Stop and pick her up along the way. Take her out to some secluded place and remind her why she married you."

"Ace." Crystal couldn't help herself. The elderly man was a leader in the church community.

The man laughed. "Don't worry, I'm not offended. I love this guy," he said, throwing his arm around Ace. "He makes me feel young, makes me think I still have possibilities. And I think I will give this little car a test drive. Send Bill on in," he said.

"How can your father compete with that?" Crystal whispered to Fiona.

"He can't. And I don't think he wants to."

Crystal gave her friend a confused look.

"He'd like to hire Ace," Fiona said.

"Oh, that's never going to work. You know that Ace's mother worked for Ford. It would be a slap in the face for him to end up doing the same thing."

"You can't deny that Ace has some great ideas. He's the consummate salesman."

Crystal looked over at Ace and found him staring at her, sending her a speculative smile. As if her appearance was giving him wild ideas, sexy ideas. Was he eyeing the top buttons of her blouse? Her breath stopped, her heart sped up, her mouth went dry. In that moment, with that smile, he could have sold her anything.

"And Ace has the right idea," Fiona said, looking around at the other cars in the showroom, seemingly unaware that her half brother was making love to Crystal with his eyes. "Have fun. Try something new. These cars are here to test-drive. You know what? I want to drive that one."

Crystal directed her gaze to where her friend was pointing. In the corner of the showroom, bigger than life, was a convertible. A custom job. Long, cobalt-blue and sleek. It practically begged to be driven.

"Yeah, that looks like just the ticket. Would you get Ace?" Fiona said, licking her lips in anticipation.

"Fiona," Crystal warned. She didn't want to approach Ace right now. She didn't trust herself—or him.

"No need to get me. I'm here, darlin'," Ace said, his voice low and clear at Crystal's shoulder, his breath whispering through the strands of her hair. A delicious shiver rippled through her.

"Fiona, uh, she wants to test-drive that car," Crystal managed to say in a choked voice. "We…we just came to tell you that we're going out for a while. I won't be home until later tonight."

That sounded so intimate, like a wife talking to her husband. Crystal felt a blush warming her cheeks.

Ace's gaze turned fierce as he studied her. "That's fine, then. No need to explain. I'm used to taking care of myself. Timmy okay?"

She nodded, unable to speak too much more with him standing this close. "He's with Grace."

She wondered how he felt about that. He and Timmy had been getting along well these past few days. Maybe too well, considering that Ace would be leaving soon. And Grace was the woman Ford had chosen over Rebecca.

But he simply nodded. "He'll be safe, then," was all he said. He frowned at Fiona. "You sure you're here because you want to drive this car?"

"What other reason?" she asked innocently.

But Crystal knew what Ace was thinking. Fiona had been intent on matching her with Ace since the man rolled into town. Still, this seemed innocent enough. Fiona certainly looked as if she wanted that car.

In less time than one would have thought, the car was out on the lot. Fiona was tying back her hair.

"Hop in," she said to Crystal and Ace, motioning to the back seat.

Ace raised one brow. He exchanged a look with Crystal.

Uh-oh, it looked like Fiona was matchmaking, after all.

But Ace only smiled and opened the door for Crystal. "No point in wasting a good opportunity to ride in one of the finest convertibles ever invented," he explained.

And Crystal had to admit that when the car took off down the highway, she felt a rush of exhilaration she'd never experienced before. Whether it was the wind trying to tug her ponytail from its clip or the fact that Ace was seated just inches away from her, she didn't know. And at this minute she didn't care.

She glanced to the side and caught Ace grinning at her.

"Like it?" he asked.

"I love it. But then, you knew I would."

She looked up to see Fiona eyeing her in the rear-view mirror.

"You behave yourself with Ace," Fiona teased, and, looking at Ace, Crystal felt like an awkward and nervous teenager again. "Don't try to do anything just because you're back there alone with him."

Crystal frowned. "Fiona, did you really want to test-drive this car?"

Fiona smiled. "Of course I did."

Crystal looked at Ace. "Of course she did," he said, but of course he and Crystal both knew in that moment what Fiona had really had in mind. Especially when she took a turn just a bit too fast and only Crystal's seat belt kept her from sliding across the seat into Ace. As it was, she slid as far as the belt would allow, which still put her closer to Ace than was probably wise. She glanced to her side and found him studying her from hooded eyes.

"You sell lots of convertibles?" Crystal asked, searching for something, anything to keep her from wondering what that look in his eyes meant.

"More than a few," he said quietly. "It's a car for those who are feeling…adventurous."

A smile played at the corners of his mouth, and she got the distinct impression that he was feeling adventurous right now.

Fiona turned another corner and Crystal slipped back the other way—and so did Ace. He slid his hand along the back of the seat and caught her shoulder to keep her from hitting the side of the car.

Now they were touching. She thought she heard Fiona sigh, but she wasn't really sure because she was looking into Ace's eyes, eyes that were filled with worry.

Eventually the car stopped rolling and Fiona got out. "Okay, that's enough for now. You two have a good time tonight," she said. "Oh, look at that. I see my husband over there. Guess he got off work early, after all." And she crossed the street to where Clay was waiting, arms crossed, a big grin on his face.

"I'll keep her busy tonight," he promised Ace as he kissed his wife, helped her into his car and drove away.

Silence fell. Crystal knew she should get out. Fiona had stopped the convertible and gotten out at Crystal's home. But the sun was beating down gently on her hair, the light breeze soothed, the convertible's upholstery was extra plush and comfortable, and Ace was only inches away.

She turned her head to look at him. "Hmm, Fiona's usually a bit more subtle than this."

"I don't think she was aiming for subtle. I have a feeling my little sister is getting frustrated with us." He smiled at her and stroked her shoulder lightly.

A shiver went through her. She couldn't help studying his mouth, his wonderfully masculine mouth. He leaned closer.

She wanted to reach out and brush the sensitive pads of her fingertips over his lips. She wanted to wrap her arms around him and pull him down beside her into the cushions of the roomy seat, to let the breeze tease the air above them as they touched. She wanted his mouth over hers, his taste on her tongue.

Her hand was on the seat-belt clasp. His, too.

A car drove past, reminding her that they were still parked on the street in front of her house and that it was still light outside.

She swallowed.

He swore. "We don't have to do this, you know."

"Just because Fiona wants it, we don't have to go along," she agreed, wishing he would move closer, hoping he wouldn't.

"Even if *we* want it, we don't have to go along," he said. And then he smiled. He kissed her once softly and then immediately pulled away. He smiled again.

Her breath slipped out of her in a long sigh of resignation, and she sat up straighter, unclipped her seat belt and placed her hand on the door handle. "Well, she almost got her way, didn't she?"

"It was a good plan, using the convertible. I've been known to say that it's my favorite in the showroom."

"She would know that. Fiona knows people."

"But," he said, climbing from the car and circling around to help her out. "Everything's fine. We haven't really touched."

"Not really," she agreed, assuming he didn't count that one swift soft kiss. It was the kind of kiss he probably bestowed on everyone, not just her. He wouldn't have expected a reaction and would probably be surprised to know that the brief caress had made her heart pound so fast she had an urge to cover it with her hand to mute the sound.

"Fiona's going to be so disappointed that we didn't fall right in line," Crystal said as they moved together toward the door.

He followed her inside as she opened the door. His body, so close behind hers, set her nerves to singing. She suddenly realized that they were completely alone tonight. Fiona had planned that, too.

"Maybe you should go home tonight so that Fiona will know for sure that nothing happened," she whispered.

"Maybe I should, but I'm not leaving you alone."

"I'll be fine."

"I know that, because I'm staying."

"Really, no," she said. "I admit that I went along with it, but not because I was worried about me. I was worried about Timmy, but he's with Grace tonight. I'm glad he's with Grace. He loves her, and he doesn't get to see her as much as he'd like. Even though she's not related, she's always found a special place for him in her heart.''

"She seems like a very nice lady."

"She is. I think she tries to be a grandmother to Timmy because she knows he hasn't got one. I'm so grateful. I worry about him.''

Ace knew that he could walk away now. The moment of passion had passed. He was free, and so was she. But in its place was this…something he couldn't ignore. Crystal looked up at him, and he saw an emotion she usually kept hidden, that longing to make up for all the things her son had missed in his life. But for this moment, in Ace's presence, she was letting go of the brave and happy front she kept up for Timmy's sake.

"You give him all he needs," he said softly. "He's never going to forget that, you know. He'll grow up and know that you tried to make up for the things he couldn't have.''

She looked up then, straight into his eyes, her own lightly misted. "I know he won't blame me, but…I just want so much for him. I want him to be happy, completely happy. Still, I know there are times and there will be times when he's going to realize that other kids have things he doesn't, and that breaks my heart.''

Glancing to the side, she turned from him. To hide the even deeper feeling in her eyes, he was sure.

It made him ache, this knowledge that she hurt and tried so hard to hide it, and he realized that this was the one thing he couldn't protect himself from. He could hold back his passion when passion was all that was at stake, even passion of such intensity he knew nothing like it. But he couldn't hold back his need to comfort her, to hold her, to help her.

He stepped closer and slid his hands up her arms.

"Come here," he said, and he tilted his head and kissed her softly. He licked at the few tears that had escaped her lashes.

A low sob escaped her throat. "I'm ashamed," she said, and tried to turn her head.

"Don't be. You're human, and you're a mother. And these past ten days have been tough and unnerving. It's all right to be afraid at times. It just means that you care. I just can't...I'm sorry, but I can't let you go through this thing alone." He pulled her tightly against him and, bringing his hand up to cup her jaw, kissed her slowly, reverently. Again and again.

She softened in his arms, twined her own arms around his neck. Her body molded to his.

But even so, he could feel some hesitation.

"Crystal?"

"I can't let you do this. I can't lean on you. I only have me to depend on. I have to be strong."

"Not tonight."

"Yes, tonight. When you're gone—"

"When I'm gone, I'll be gone and you'll go on as you have. But tonight I'm here with you, and you can lean on me. Just this one time. Take what I have."

She lifted her head from where she had hidden it against his body. Tears still glistened in her eyes, but there was a sense of wonder, as well. She smiled at him, slowly.

"You're a wonderful, generous man, Ace." She rose on her toes and kissed him. Softly, shyly. She pulled back, and then a sudden light, a glow, filled her face, and she kissed him again. Less softly, less shyly. She nibbled at the corners of his mouth, brushed her lips against his, kissed him fully, deeply, until the heat rose within him like an inferno, engulfing him, scorching him.

He groaned. "I'm sorry, angel," he said. "I'm sorry." Licking at the seam of her lips, he gained entrance and claimed the territory of her mouth.

It was hot, moist, tasting of mint. Crystal met him, kiss for kiss.

He urged her deeper into the entry of the house, then kicked the door shut. The closed curtains of the house encased them in shadows with just a few thin rays of sunlight intruding.

Good. He wanted no intruders this evening. If this was all of her he was to have—and it was—he would take it. Every bit, every minute, every touch and every sigh.

"You're sure?" she asked on a whisper as if she'd heard his thoughts.

"You know we've been heading toward this since that first day," he said, and he swung her into his arms, marching toward the room he'd dreamed of for long nights.

But as he laid her down on the cinnamon-and-cream-and-peaches coverlet of her bed, he hesitated. That terrible trusting look in her eyes pulled him up short.

"I don't want to hurt you." He said the words he

never remembered saying to a woman before at a moment like this. No doubt because he'd never had a woman like Crystal before.

She raised her chin and took in a deep breath, her curves shifting and making him crazy to have her. But he held back.

"You can't hurt me," she whispered. "You're a fantasy, a one-night thing, like that gorgeous blue convertible. Something to enjoy once before life overtakes you and routine catches you up. My life is filled with routine, Ace. Responsibility. Happiness, too, of course, but not much excitement. Not many fantasy moments."

A man didn't get an invitation like that from a woman like this very often. Most men would have leaped on her, taken all she had, but... She considered him a fantasy, not real. A small, insistent pain nagged him as he gazed down at her, admiring all that she was.

Well, he wasn't real, at least not for her, was he? He'd told her time and time again that he couldn't stay, and wasn't that what fantasies were? Temporary temptations. She would have a hard life ahead of her raising her son alone. He knew that better than anyone. He could give her one night; he could make a memory for himself, as well.

"If you want a fantasy, then maybe we should be a bit more adventurous than making love on the bed," he said with a grin.

She opened her eyes wide. "What would you suggest?"

He raised one shoulder. "Where's your car?"

She frowned, confused. "At the hospital. Fiona drove."

"Then your garage is empty?"

"Yes."

"Good. I'll be right back." He turned to go.

"Ace?"

"Yes?" He looked over his shoulder.

"Should I..." He could almost hear her nervous swallow. "Should I undress?"

He closed his eyes and let his head fall back against the wall as he took deep breaths. "No. Don't." The words came out choked. "If you get undressed, I won't be able to do this right, and I intend to do this right. Just wait."

He left quickly, before he could think of her naked in his arms. He gathered what he needed, did what he'd decided to do. In less than five minutes he was back.

She sat up nervously.

He circled the bed and took her hand. "Come with me."

She followed him, and he led her toward the side of the house. "Ace, this is the way to the garage."

"I know." And he slid the door open, revealed what he'd done.

The blue convertible took up almost all of the space, but he had still managed to light a dozen candles and tuck them in safe places. She didn't have any decent wine, but he had made do with what she had. Now he led her to the rear door. He opened it and motioned her inside.

And suddenly she smiled. "We're going to make

love in one of your cars. Are you sure you can do that? Can you sell it afterward?"

"I can charge double," he teased, and he maneuvered her farther in, then turned to her. He reached for the glasses of wine he had placed there and handed one to her. "To fantasies," he said.

"To blue convertibles and men named Ace," she whispered, and took a sip. When she set the glass aside, her lips were moist. He couldn't wait any longer.

"I'm going to make love to you now, darlin'," he told her.

"I'm going to let you. I'm going to touch you, too," she said.

He kissed her mouth, then placed his arm beneath her and lowered her to the cushions.

"It won't be as comfortable as a bed," he whispered over her lips.

"It's going to be wonderful," she said.

And later, as he opened the last button on her dress and bared her to his view, he knew that she was right. As he took the bud of her breast into his mouth, he knew that she was more than right.

She moaned as he suckled her. His fingers traced a line down her side, across her hip. He slid her lacy white panties off and tossed them aside, trailing his fingers through the soft curls that hid her from his view.

Her body bucked beneath his touch.

"Shh, tell me if I do anything you don't like," he whispered.

"You won't," she whispered back. "Do more."

And he did. He stroked her gently, deeply until she was wet and hot and very ready. Her eyes were dull with passion, her lips moist.

"Ace, let me touch you, too. Make you ready."

He closed his eyes as she reached for his belt buckle. In an effort to free him, she slipped delicate fingers inside the waistband of his pants, and he nearly went mad with need.

He covered her hand with his own.

"I'm more than ready, sweetheart." He gasped out the words and twisted against her slightly so she could feel just how ready he was.

For half a second he thought he saw her smile as she nodded and moved back slightly. He unzipped his pants, relieving the pressure. He allowed her to unbutton his shirt, though her butterfly touches drove him wild.

"Oh, lady, I want you." He almost didn't recognize his own voice.

"I want you to remember this," she whispered, peeling the last of his clothes from him and skimming her hands down his body.

"Nothing could make me forget this." He stroked his fingertips across her lips, down her jaw, skimming the outline of her breast, barely brushing her nipple. "Let me make it memorable for *you*. Real memorable," he said, teasing the indentation of her waist and slowly, very slowly slipping his fingers into her depths.

She cried out and raised herself to him.

"Ace!" Her voice was high and breathy.

"Yes," he agreed harshly, and he joined his body

to hers, and the breath and all his will left his body. She was his entire focus, his every need.

Slowly he took her until she whimpered with need and his own body begged for release and he couldn't go slowly anymore. But he wanted her with him. He had to have her with him. To share as they'd been sharing these past few days.

"Now, darlin'," he said. "With me."

"Yes, with you," she said on a sob, and then the stars spilled into his senses and he collapsed against Crystal's soft, warm body.

Long moments later he realized that he must be crushing her, and he lifted her into his arms, turned with her as much as he could in the small space so that he was the one beneath.

She looked so beautiful, so fragile in the pale glow of the candles. This night he had meant to give her a fantasy. Instead, she had given him one.

He smiled against her hair, and then he frowned, remembering that he had almost forgotten protection until they were both naked and almost past the point of no return. She had looked suddenly nervous, biting her lip, haltingly confessing that she didn't have any birth control. He had cursed himself as he stopped to look for what he should have had at hand in the first place.

How could he, of all people, have forgotten that? How could he have made her have to ask?

He pulled her closer.

"It won't happen again, darlin'," he promised.

She tensed, and he realized what she was thinking.

"I won't let you worry about protection again," he said.

He could feel her smile against his skin. "Well, we did say it would be just this one time," she said.

Like hell. "Maybe just this one night." He turned her in his arms and kissed her.

"Kiss me back," he urged.

And she did. Later, back in her room, in her bed she took him to heaven again, too. It was a night to remember. He knew he'd never know another like it in his lifetime. Just as he knew that the morning would come too soon.

Fantasies had a way of looking different in the morning light.

Eleven

Ace had held her close all night, sometimes so closely that she almost didn't have room to breathe. When he realized he was doing that, he always awoke and apologized, guilt filling his eyes. She wondered how many times in his life he'd wanted to hold on to things, how many times he'd wanted his father, acceptance, the overtures of friends, instead of the sneers of those who considered him an interloper. Too many times, she guessed, and she was pretty certain that he had always backed away, eased up, just as he'd eased up on holding her too tightly.

She understood that kind of dilemma, because *she* was beginning to want to hold on to him, and it just wouldn't do.

When he awoke the next morning and looked into her eyes, she sensed a kind of wariness, a carefulness.

"Are you all right?" he asked.

No, she would never be all right. Now that she knew how things could be, she would never be satisfied with less again. But she was going to have to learn to live dissatisfied.

"I'm good," she lied. "I'd better go call Grace." She made her exit from the bedroom as quickly as she could. If that wasn't goodbye looming in his eyes, she didn't know what was. He was getting to the end of his mission here. Mission Creek Motors was making Lone Star Autos look bad. He had shown his father that he could be a success without Carson money or influence. He had given his father a run for his money and won. It was all he had come for, and he wouldn't want to stay around looking like a wanna-be.

She half hoped that he'd come after her, coax her back into bed. But he didn't. Soon after, she heard him getting ready for work.

He peeked in on her as she was making breakfast. She couldn't quite meet his gaze. "Everything's almost ready here. I'll leave it covered on the stove to keep warm. I'm going to go pick up Timmy now."

"I could get him if you want," he offered, but when she looked at him, she saw concern in his eyes and knew that he was worrying that she would expect something of him, the way John had. The way her father had always said that her mother expected too much and then had walked out the door. She knew how it was. Nothing lasted forever, maybe not even more than one night.

That was okay, she thought, squaring her shoulders. She'd known how it would be; she'd even told him how it would be. It wasn't his fault that the night had changed her more than she'd thought it would.

She managed a smile, a strong, genuine smile. Ace was a good man. Her needs weren't his concern, but if he thought she was hurting, *he* would hurt. He'd want to help her, and this was one thing he couldn't help her with.

"Have a good day. Sell lots of cars. Be happy." She couldn't seem to keep from saying that last.

Immediately his concerned look deepened. He snagged her around the waist and pulled her close.

The need for him was almost overwhelming. Her throat nearly closed, and she had to shut her eyes to keep him from seeing the distress there.

"Something's wrong," he whispered.

But somehow she managed to shake her head and keep herself from begging him to stay with her. She pasted on her old trusted smile again.

"I just didn't get enough sleep," she said, keeping it light. "Some of us are used to going to bed early."

"You should stay home and take care of yourself today," he said. "I could take care of you."

It sounded like heaven. It sounded much too tempting. If she spent too much time alone with him now, she'd end up telling him all sorts of things, imagining all sorts of things. If she wasn't careful, she was going to start believing she was falling in love with him. And that was the last thing on earth she wanted. A relationship with a charming wanderer who could commit to no one? Not for her. Not for a woman with a child.

She wrinkled her nose and chuckled. "Um, sounds nice, but no. I've got to go."

She forced herself to push away from him and leave. She was pretty sure it was time to send Ace back to the Overton Apartments. Having him here after last night just wasn't going to work.

Besides, Branson, or whoever had been following her and Timmy, seemed to have given up the pursuit.

* * *

If ever a woman wanted him out of her life, it was Crystal Bennett, Ace thought, watching her giving him her tenth anxious look of the day. It had been two days since they'd made love, and she was showing increasing signs of regret.

He was feeling regret, too, although of a different nature. He wanted her smiles back. Her real smiles. Not those fake polite ones she threw his way every so often. As incredible as making love to her had been, he would have been willing to go back and undo that night if doing so would bring back her smiles and leave her happy. He had to know she would be happy when he left Mission Creek.

That didn't mean he'd stopped wanting to touch her. What had been a longing, a desire before was like a constant roaring and hungry bonfire within him now.

But touching her had made her unhappy. That was very clear, and he wasn't going to do it again if he could help it.

He probably should get out of here, go back to the apartments or even leave town. There really wasn't much reason to stay. He'd come here filled with anger and a need to exact some sort of retribution, to make a point. He supposed that he had, in a sense. Mission Creek Motors had ten times the business Lone Star Auto had these days, but the sense of satisfaction, of closure that he'd thought he'd feel had never materialized. He knew now that it probably never would. Nothing was ever really going to change the past or make up for it.

No doubt he should just accept that, cut his losses and leave. Move on to the next town and the next job. Things seemed to have died down here. No one had approached Crystal or Timmy. There really wasn't any reason to stay.

He was telling himself just that when the phone rang later that night. Crystal was putting Timmy to bed. She was busy doing the most important work of her life—caring for her child. And that child was sleepy. He needed his rest, not an interruption.

Ace picked up the phone.

"Hello. Bennett residence," he said.

No response. Not even the sound of someone breathing.

"Hello?" he said again.

Still no answer. Probably a wrong number. He was talking to a dead phone.

Then he heard the click, the sound of the connection being severed at the other end of the line.

A wrong number. Definitely. Or maybe a man calling. Surely men called her now and then, men who wouldn't care to hear another man answering the phone.

Ace was amazed at the swift feeling of possessiveness that enveloped him, a savage need to put up barriers and keep all other men out. He fought it. Inch by inch, sensation by sensation, he tamed it. Slowly. Very slowly until it seemed as if he might have the thing licked and under some semblance of control.

A man calling Crystal, wanting to ask her out.

Maybe he didn't have complete control over himself as yet. And maybe that hadn't been a man wanting to ask Crystal out. Maybe it had been a man wanting to threaten her, to see if she was home alone.

Carefully Ace hung up the phone, fighting the sick sensation of fear that assaulted him.

He was staying awhile longer. Nothing could drag him away yet. He was going to turn his efforts to making sure she would be safe and protected when he did go. That was his new goal, and a much worthier one than the reason he had come here in the first place.

He had lived his life with missing pieces, knowing he had been tossed aside, but he had, at least, always been safe.

If it took all he had, all the power he could draw on, all the will, he was going to make Crystal safe.

She came out of the room with a smile on her face, the same smile she'd been wearing for days, the pretend smile she wore for his sake.

"Who was that?" she asked.

Well, two could play at this game of pretend, he thought, knowing that nothing could make him reveal his suspicions.

"Salesman," he said. "You know how pushy those guys can be." He gave her a grin.

Her answering chuckle was genuine, so sweet and special that he wanted to catch it somehow, pack it up so that he could take it with him and keep it for the weeks and years ahead when he would be alone again and would want to remember her.

He would always remember her.

"How's Timmy?"

Immediately her smile faded. "I don't know. His

friend Benny has upset him. Benny, it seems, is visiting his grandfather's farm. Timmy would love to do something like that, but...he doesn't have a grandfather. Not a real one. Hard to argue that point, isn't it?''

"So what are you going to do?"

She shrugged. "I don't know. Take him out to Carson Ranch again, I think. He was just there with Grace, but he usually stays at the house. I thought I might get Flynt to give him his first ride on a pony.''

"Flynt's a busy man.''

"I know that.'' Immediately hurt crept into her eyes. He cursed himself for putting that there.

"I didn't mean that he wouldn't do that for Timmy. I only meant...well, I know a few things about horses, and I think Timmy trusts me. It can be a scary business mounting your first horse. That is, well, I was a lot older than he is and already away at the academy when I first tried it. It helps if the person with you is someone you trust. Maybe I...'' He stopped, embarrassed to think that he was babbling. He, who'd made his reputation by selling his way into situations.

"Are you volunteering to go out to Carson Ranch and help Timmy with his first horseback ride?''

It sounded foolish, ridiculous. "Yeah, I suppose that was a crazy idea. A ranch that size has any number of people capable of helping a small boy learn the ropes.''

She shook her head. "Not someone Timmy trusts, though. And Flynt or Matt might do it, but like you said, they're busy men. It would be an imposition. You're willing to go out there?''

For some reason he was desperate to go out there, but it was the last thing he wanted to admit to. No need to, anyway, he decided as a perfectly valid excuse came to him. He smiled. "It would be the height of brazenness, wouldn't it? To chip away at the Carson auto business and then march onto Carson land as if I belonged there?"

"It would probably bring a lot of Carsons running to see," she warned. She gave him a slow smile and crossed her arms.

And he knew suddenly and without a doubt that he'd been had by a woman whose sweet eyes revealed nothing but good intentions. Oh, he knew what she was thinking. She'd staged that dinner the other day in the hopes that he and his family would...well, that they'd become a family. She was still at it.

Never gonna happen, sweetheart, he thought. This plan won't work any better than the last. But it *would* give him the opportunity for one last grand parting shot.

More importantly, he would be the one to get to introduce Timmy to his first horse. Ace was amazed, maybe even ashamed and definitely alarmed at the sense of possessiveness he felt. But there was no denying it. He wanted to be the man who put Timmy on a horse, no one else. He wanted it done right. Nothing scary and no chance that Timmy could get hurt.

"I'd be honored if you'd let me do this," he told her.

She stood there quietly, just gazing at him. Finally

she nodded. "It will be a good way to end things," she said softly.

Something shifted deep inside him. Something uncomfortable and painful. "We're ending things, then, are we?"

Crystal met his eyes and nodded slowly. "I think we have to, don't you? For Timmy, at least."

He knew what she meant. She didn't want her son getting too attached to him, getting hurt if he stuck around too long.

"You're right," he said. "We'll do this, then I'll be gone soon afterward."

He had better make sure that she was safe, and fast. At the very least, he needed to make sure that there was someone to watch over her after he was gone.

Ace had done a lot of horseback riding in his life. Crystal could see that from the start. It was more than the jeans, the boots and the hat that looked like it had endured years of wear. It was the way he felt at ease with the animals and they with him.

"Thank you for letting us bring Timmy out to the ranch," she told Flynt as she watched Ace saddling and soothing a little dappled pony named Freckles.

Flynt shifted uncomfortably. "You and Timmy are always welcome, you know that."

She smiled. "I do, but you know that's not what I meant." She looked purposefully toward Ace.

Flynt shrugged. "You think Josie would have let me in the house tonight if I hadn't? I have to say that it goes against the grain inviting a man to my house who's made every effort to run Dad out of business.

Still, I have to give him credit. He's got the guts of a Carson. And he knows how to flirt with a horse. Makes the animal feel comfortable."

He was making her son feel comfortable, too, Crystal acknowledged a few minutes later when Ace came to fetch Timmy from her.

He gave Flynt a curt nod. "Good stock," he said, motioning toward the horse. "He'll make a fine mount for a young cowboy."

It was the closest thing to a compliment Ace had paid a Carson in all his time here in Mission Creek.

Flynt stared back and nodded.

"Carson stock is the best."

"Of course."

"You handled that pony like a Carson. Must be in the blood."

Ace appeared to mull that comment over. "I had a good teacher at the academy."

Crystal expected Flynt to get angry at Ace for apparently still considering it an insult to be called a Carson. Instead, he laughed. "You don't give an inch, do you?"

Ace looked to the side for a long time. Finally he shook his head. "Look, I know you're not responsible for my life, but the years I was growing up I didn't know who my father was. He might have been a bank robber or worse. I couldn't live worrying about my genetics or what I was destined to be because of an accident of birth. I was taught that I had to be my own man, and that's what I've tried to be. Again, not your fault, but don't expect me to jump on the Carson bandwagon and pretend to be one when I've never been one before."

The two men squared off, standing there staring at each other. Finally Flynt nodded. "You argue real well, too, big brother. Looks like you had good teachers there, too."

The closest thing to a smile played about Ace's lips. "My mother was a special woman. She insisted I learn a few things. And my stepfather was a very wise man. I tried to do them justice. Guess I fall down in the manners department now and then, though. Thanks for letting me near your horses."

Flynt opened his mouth.

Ace raised a brow and Flynt laughed. "All right, I won't say that you're a Carson."

"That's best. You ready, wildcat?" Ace asked Timmy.

Crystal looked down at her son, who was still holding her hand. More tightly now. He nodded, but his eyes grew huge when he looked at the pony. "Big."

Ace sank to one knee beside him.

"Maybe he is, but that's not his fault. He can't help it. Besides, he's not so big we can't handle him." Ace held out his arms. "Come on, wildcat, you and me together."

Timmy let go of Crystal's hand and stepped forward, allowing Ace to swing him high and carry him off.

"Ace?" Crystal asked.

He turned and winked at her. "Don't worry, little mother. His life is golden. I won't let anything happen to him. That's a solemn promise, and I don't, as you know, make many promises."

She knew, and hot tears rose in her throat. She choked them back and thought she heard Flynt swear beside her.

"He doesn't like us very much, does he."

She sighed. "He had a hard beginning. Lessons you learn in childhood are hard to forget."

Flynt looked down at Crystal. She knew she hadn't disguised the worry in her voice very well, but he nodded toward Ace. "I wouldn't worry. That boy is loved and wanted by everyone he meets, even if his father didn't have the sense of Freckles there."

Crystal knew that what he said was most likely true. She also knew she shouldn't interfere in Ace's life or in Flynt's. Some things weren't her business.

"I don't think that Ace had much love outside of his mother when he was young. He went to school in an academy where he was made to feel like an outsider every day. It's stuck with him. Maybe forever."

Flynt didn't say anything for a long time. At last he nodded. "I love my father, Crystal."

"He's a good man," she said. "But even good men make mistakes that change lives forever. It's going to be difficult to win Ace over."

"But you think we should make an effort to win him over." The man beside her turned suddenly to look at her. "This business with Timmy, whose idea was it?"

She looked up at him innocently. "Timmy wanted to visit a ranch. This one was convenient. I don't know why Ace objected when I told him I was going to ask *you* to teach Timmy to ride."

Flynt smiled. "You are a devious woman, Crystal."

She smiled back, but then she sighed. "Still, it doesn't look like it's working, does it? He and Timmy are doing just great, but he's still fighting the Carsons. I just don't want him to leave Mission Creek thinking he always has to be alone. It would be good if he made some sort of a connection with your family."

Flynt looked back over his shoulder. "Well, it looks like you're not alone. Here come Fiona and Cara and Ma. Matt, too. Bringing food out for a picnic. The battle to win Ace over is still on, I'd say."

Within minutes the Carson women had engaged Flynt and Matt's help and had set up a table groaning with food. By the time Ace had finished Timmy's lesson and was heading toward Crystal's way to return her son to her, everything was waiting.

Crystal looked at Ace and saw the moment he noticed what was going on. He stopped in his tracks.

"Come on, Ace. Eat," Timmy commanded, pulling Ace toward the group.

But a mask had come down over Ace's eyes. He nodded politely to the women. He was poised to make some excuse and get out of there, Crystal knew.

"Stay, Ace," she said quietly, and he looked down into her eyes. For a moment it was as if no one else was even there. Every fiber in his body was ready for flight. She could see it, feel it, even taste it in the air.

"Please, stay," she said again, and those blue eyes grew sad. They softened.

Grace appeared at his elbow. "Please stay," the soft-voiced woman said. "We would be so honored to have your company."

The sadness in his eyes grew, but he turned to Grace. "I'm the one who would be honored, ma'am." Crystal knew that Ace's I-will-harm-no-woman attitude held a special place for Grace. She suspected that he felt sorry for Grace's having endured years of marriage to Ford Carson. Not exactly what she was hoping for, but it got him moving to wash his hands and sit down.

"Did you have fun, sweetie?" she asked Timmy as she led him to the table.

"Yep. Ace hepped me," he said, then stuck a biscuit in his mouth.

She turned toward Ace. "Thank you," she whispered. "I was worried about his first time."

But then, Ace was good at first times, wasn't he, she thought, remembering the first time they'd made love the other day.

She couldn't help blushing. He raised one brow and smiled at her. Surely he couldn't know what she was thinking.

The conversation flowed around them. The Carsons tried to get Ace's attention. He was polite but mostly silent. Still, he stayed, Crystal noted. He didn't contribute to the conversation, but he didn't attempt to leave, either. He seemed almost…content.

And then she felt him stiffen at her side.

She looked up and turned.

Ford was approaching.

It was, at that moment, as if all the air and noise

in the world was sucked into a void. The silence wasn't the good kind.

Then Grace bustled forward. She took her husband's hand and drew him toward a place at the opposite end of the table.

Ford sat, but he didn't pick up a fork. He simply stared down the table toward his oldest son.

Crystal wanted to reach out and take Ace's hand, but she was pretty sure he wouldn't appreciate that now. He needed to face his father unassisted.

"Ace was just teaching Timmy to ride," Fiona said, smiling at her father.

"He's a good horseman," Cara put in.

"Damn good," Matt and Flynt said together, as if they'd planned it.

Ace looked like a cold, silent statue.

Ford's eyes grew sadder. He glanced around the table. As if he'd given some sort of silent signal, one by one his family members rose.

"Got to get back to work," Flynt said.

"Yeah, ain't it the truth?" Matt agreed as he drifted away.

Fiona and Cara exchanged a look. "Come on, sis, we're outta here. Ace, Crystal, Timmy," Fiona said.

Crystal started to rise, too.

Automatically Ace reached out and touched her hand briefly. "Stay," he said quietly. "I have no secrets."

She looked at Timmy. Grace scooped him up. "I think I've got some special cookies in the kitchen," she said, and Timmy smiled up at her.

"I'll stay," Crystal whispered.

Within a minute, only Ford, Crystal and Ace remained.

"The two of you are an item?" Ford asked.

Ace studied his father. "Not that it's any of your concern, but we're friends."

Crystal knew what he meant and so did Ford. Ace would not be repeating his father's mistakes.

Ford nodded.

"You had something to say," Ace said. "Go ahead and say it."

Ford didn't look away. Instead, he lifted his head higher and stared directly into his son's eyes. "You don't like me, and I don't blame you. I didn't do right by your mother. Even if I didn't know she was pregnant when she left, even if I didn't know that my father had run her off, I should have been man enough to follow up and make sure that she wasn't carrying my child. Later, after I had Flynt, I did try to find her, but my father had hid her well, I guess. Or maybe even that wasn't true. I was happy, and I was afraid of what I'd find, what I'd done. I was a coward, I guess. Eventually, though, I got older, the years touched me, and I looked harder. I found out where she was. I heard that you had been born. I went there and saw you."

Ace looked as if he'd turned to stone. "You saw me where?"

"In your front yard. Many years after your birth. You were with your stepfather. It was clear that he loved you and you loved him. I...I didn't know what to do. Honesty and honor directed me to step forward, but you looked happy with him. It didn't seem fair or right to try to worm my way into your life after so many years had passed. It didn't seem fair to you or to him or even to Rebecca. I saw you, and I decided that seeing you once would have to be enough. I never went back.''

Crystal went with her instincts this time. To hell with Ford and the world and her inhibitions. She covered Ace's hand with hers. Instantly he wrapped his fingers around hers. She wondered if he was even aware that he did it. His grip was so strong, his hand so cold.

"Was it?" Ace asked. "Was it enough?" He stood and Crystal rose with him. He stared down at Ford.

Ford rose to his feet. "It wasn't enough," he said in a voice that was barely above a whisper. "It was too much." Then he sat down heavily. Like a stone falling.

Crystal moved forward. "Ace, he's been ill in the past. His heart."

Ace stared at his father, and the expression in his eyes was unreadable, deep and terrible and aching. "I'll call a doctor," he said tightly.

He walked away at a quick clip.

Crystal longed to run after him, but she couldn't leave Ford here alone. Of course Ace had needed to go. He'd had to call.

Then Grace was flying outside.

"I'm okay," Ford said. "I'm fine." He looked up at Crystal. "Go. Don't let him be alone. I think there's been enough of that. *I've* done enough of that."

Crystal didn't have to be asked twice. She only

stopped to turn to Grace, her question about Timmy on her lips.

"He's napping," Grace said. "I've got someone watching him. I'll call you when he's up."

Crystal ran to and then through the house. She ran toward the car that she and Ace had come in. He was sitting in the front seat, his body rigid, his face set in grim lines.

She opened the door and climbed in.

Ace pulled her across the seat and onto his lap. He kissed her hard. Two times. Three. Fiercely. Desperately. She felt all the pain that lay deep within him rising to the surface.

"I'm sorry," she said. "I wanted you to have family. I wanted you to get to know them."

He brushed her hair back and kissed her throat. "I know. I know you did. I knew what you were doing, and I let you do it, but..."

She raised her head and framed his face with her hands as she looked into those intense blue eyes.

"But?" she prompted.

"But don't do it anymore," he said. "We both know I'm not staying. I'm not staying, Crystal, and when I leave here, I leave here alone. No family ties. No anything."

She nodded then and kissed him. "No anything," she agreed.

And her words were like a death knell, a final cutting of the cord that bound them.

"No anything," he repeated, and when he kissed her this time, it was slow and sweet and sad.

They had started their long goodbye. Now all that was left were the final details and the leaving.

Twelve

She wanted to end it. Ace still couldn't get that thought out of his mind two days later, even though by rights he ought to be thinking about other things. Like the fact that Dan Foyerre had returned a car to him.

It should have bothered him. He had made a business out of delivering what he promised to his customers and, of course, he had agreed to the return even though J.D. had fumed. But it just hadn't affected him that much.

Crystal, on the other hand, was severely distressed. "That's no way to treat you," she said as she cleared away the breakfast dishes. "Even Dan admits that there's nothing wrong with the car, that it was just what he wanted, and that you offered him the best deal. What was the problem?"

Ace smiled as she paced, her hazel eyes flashing. "You know he's a friend of Ford's. He found himself with a guilty conscience, it seems. You can't fault a man for being loyal to his friends." Not even if that friend was Ford Carson.

She sank in a heap on a chair. "I know. I'm surprised he bought the car at all. Guess it just shows what a good salesman you are," she said, giving him one of her beautiful smiles. "But still, he should have thought of his loyalty to Ford before, not after, he bought the car. Now you're the one paying the price. I know J.D.'s ways. You can't tell me he's not giving you grief."

He loved that she was defending him and worrying about him. Except he didn't want her worrying about him. Twice now she'd thrown him together with his half brothers and sisters, trying to forge a bond between them. She wanted him to have a family, and his siblings didn't seem averse to the idea. Not that Ace understood why. He certainly hadn't given them any encouragement. He wished that he could, if only to make Crystal happy. He wanted to remember her smiling and content when he left, and they'd both agreed that he was indeed going.

All that was left was to make sure that Crystal was safe. That was the only reason he was still standing here today.

"Ace?"

He smiled down at her, realizing that he hadn't answered her comment about how his employer was treating him.

"Don't worry. J.D. is mostly hot air," he assured her. Besides, it didn't much matter, Ace couldn't help admitting. Soon Ace would just be last week's gossip in Mission Creek. Soon J.D. and even Crystal would fade into memory.

But even as he thought it, he looked into her lovely eyes and knew that her memory would take a long time to fade.

"I'd better go to work," he said.

"I thought you weren't worried about J.D. and his opinions," she said, looking unconvinced.

He shrugged. "A man has to have a good opinion of himself, too," he said with a grin.

For some reason, that didn't make her smile, as he'd intended. If anything, the worry in her eyes increased.

"How do you feel about Dan returning the car, then?" she asked softly. "I know how hard you've worked."

He touched her cheek gently. "I feel like I don't want you worrying about me. There's no need."

Even though he was very worried about *her*. There shouldn't have been a need. There had been no more strange phone calls, no more strangers visiting the day-care center. No one had had even a glimpse of Branson Hines for days.

And that was what scared him, Ace thought three hours later, standing in his showroom on this sunny day. Where in hell was the man?

The question had nagged him for days.

But at that moment he looked out the plate-glass window and saw Flynt and Matt pull up outside the dealership. Cara and Fiona pulled up beside them.

When they got out, he saw that Crystal was in the back seat.

Ace raised a brow. Interesting. "Must be lunch hour," he said to J.D., looking down at his watch. "Hope you've got enough food in the back to feed the Carsons."

J.D. frowned. "The Carsons," he said with disgust.

For the first time Ace felt a trace of annoyance at

J.D.'s attitude. In fact, he felt more than a trace of annoyance when he remembered how Fiona had opened up to him from the first and how Flynt and Matt and Cara had ignored his bad temper. He especially felt disgruntled when he remembered what a friend his half siblings had been to Crystal and Timmy.

"They're not so bad," he was surprised to hear himself saying. "You just have to get to know them." Besides, his siblings were not and had never been responsible for what had happened to his mother and himself.

He opened the door to them.

"Hi, Ace," Cara said, giving him a smile as she stepped in. "Mind if we look around?"

"You want to look at cars?" J.D. asked, his eyes opening wide.

"That *is* what you sell, isn't it, J.D.?" Fiona asked.

The man practically rubbed his hands together with glee. "Yes, of course. What would you like to see?"

Fiona shrugged. "Oh, I don't know yet. I'll let my big brother help me decide. You'll do that, won't you, Ace?"

Ace looked at Fiona and Cara, and his mouth lifted slightly at the corners. "You've come to Mission Creek Motors to look for a car."

Cara and Fiona turned to Crystal. "Is there something wrong with all the men here?" Cara asked. "What do they think we've come here to buy? Lunch?"

Crystal chuckled. "I think you'd better show them something quickly, Ace. They're getting a bit testy."

He turned his gaze on her. She looked far too innocent.

"You didn't happen to mention the name Dan Foyerre to them, did you?" he asked.

Her eyes widened. "Why would I do that?" she asked. But he didn't fail to notice that she held her body a bit more rigidly than usual. Didn't she know that an innocent like her couldn't lie to a man like him?

He smiled down at her. "It's all right, darlin'. I don't mind selling my sisters a car if they really want one."

But at that moment, Matt and Flynt came up behind him. "Now, what I want to know," Matt was saying, gesturing to a long stylish silver cruiser, "is just how this thing handles. And how safe it is. It looks like something I'd feel comfortable letting Rose drive, but I need to know the details. What extra features does it have that will help protect my wife when she's out on the road?"

Ace and Flynt exchanged a look.

"You came to me to buy a car for your wife?"

Flynt held out his hands palms up. "Can't blame a man for wanting the safest car for his woman, can you?" he asked. "A man might go…just anywhere looking for the safest vehicle."

"And this doesn't have anything to do with Dan Foyerre?" Ace eyed his brothers.

"Who?" Matt asked, even though Ace knew that Dan had been an old Carson-family friend for years.

He couldn't help chuckling. "Never mind me," he said. "I'm just a hardheaded…Carson."

"Lot of those around," Fiona said.

His brothers and sisters gathered around. Ace did his best not to sell them anything, but they were having none of it. Before they had left, every single one of them had bought a car.

"Omar will love this," Cara said, patting Ace on the cheek. "Come on, Fiona, Crystal."

"Wait," Ace said, and every Carson in the place stared at him. "Thank you," he said. "I know I've been a jerk."

"Oh," Fiona said, lifting a shoulder, "any Carson would have been just as much of a jerk. We're all a bit hardheaded and stubborn at times."

That drew a laugh from the few other customers in the dealership.

Ace smiled at his little sister. "You won't mind waiting for Crystal a few minutes, will you?" he asked. "She and I need to talk. Just for a minute."

Cara and Fiona looked mutinous.

"I wouldn't be angry at her just because she told my secrets and brought you here," he said, furrowing his brow. "You should know that."

They looked suitably subdued. They waved and called goodbye, following Matt and Flynt out the door and leaving Crystal behind.

Ace reached for her hand. Gently he drew her into the office at the back of the dealership. Another salesman was already there.

Ace frowned. "I need a bit of privacy, Bob," he said. The man looked at Crystal. Ace could see that he was trying not to smile.

"Sure thing," Bob said, making a quick exit.

The door had barely shut behind the man when Ace took Crystal in his arms. His lips came down on hers in a hard kiss.

"You've got to stop," he said softly, his lips still resting against hers.

She kissed him back. "Kissing you?" she whispered, and then kissed him again. "I wasn't the one who started it."

He smiled against her skin. "You've got to stop trying to protect me from the Carsons. And stop trying to get all of us together."

She pulled back from him then and gazed up into his eyes, that deeply troubled look cutting off his breath. "They're nice people," she said gently. "They want to know you, want to claim you."

He traced his fingers down her cheek, tucked his thumb beneath her chin. "They're nice people," he agreed, "but there are holes in our history and parts of our past that I don't want to open up. Ever. My brothers and sisters and I can talk on a surface level, we can smile, we can do business and even joke, but there are parts of our life—important parts—that can't intersect. It's best not to even start. I can't stay here, Crystal. I'm going, and when I go, I don't want to leave ties or unfinished business. I don't want to…hurt anyone."

She reached up then and framed his face with her hands.

"I know that," she said solemnly. "And I want you to know I'm doing my best not to get hurt."

"Good." He drew her close again and kissed her deeply.

When he let her go this time, he couldn't quite manage to keep the regret from his eyes.

"Don't look like that," she said. "We both knew this was short-term. I don't want to get deeply involved. I'm not looking for marriage or forever. I just…it was just a shame for you and your siblings to be so at odds."

She kissed him lightly then on the lips, and he felt as if his soul followed her when she drew away.

"You're a very special woman, Crystal. I see now what all those people were saying when they said that you could talk anyone into giving anything. I can't believe you got a whole group of Carsons to come to Mission Creek Motors to buy cars."

She looked vaguely uncomfortable, a sweet blush coloring her cheeks. "It's usually pretty easy to get Carsons fired up about things. They all have a strong sense of justice. They're good people."

He knew she wasn't just talking about his brothers and sisters. She was talking about him.

"Really?" he asked. "And how about Bennetts? What gets them fired up about things? What gets you fired up?" He grinned down at her, then leaned in close and traced his lips along her jaw, dipping down to the pulse at the base of her throat.

She sighed against him. For a moment she melted for him, but then she lifted her head. She firmed her lips.

"It would be best if I got back to work," she finally said. "I guess the clock gets me fired up. And my son. Anything to do with my son. And anything that threatens to hurt him I can't allow in my life. Even if I want that something real bad.''

Without another word, she moved to the door.

Before she could open it, he said. ''I wouldn't hurt him. Not if I could help it.''

''I know that,'' she gazed at him with suspiciously shiny eyes. ''But sometimes we just can't help hurting a child. And that means we can't always have all the things we want.''

''We give up those things,'' he agreed, nodding. ''All right, I'll see you in a few hours, and I'll pack my things.''

But first, he thought as she left him standing there, he would make some arrangements.

Hours later, he stood beside Matt and Flynt out at Carson Ranch.

''I want her safe,'' he said. ''I wouldn't ask this otherwise.''

Flynt dared to lay a hand on his half brother's shoulder. ''You didn't need to ask, but we're glad you did. Don't worry. We'll watch over her when you've gone.''

That was good, then, Ace thought, climbing back in his car. Everything was in place. The only thing left to do was cut the ties.

Crystal stood in her office with the door closed, her hands pressed over her mouth to keep the moan from escaping.

Somehow she had managed to smile and joke with Fiona and Cara on her way back to work. Somehow she had managed to avoid thinking about how things had gotten away from her.

But here in the privacy of her office, in the accusing silence, she couldn't deny what had happened.

She had fallen in love with Ace Carson. Even while she was telling him that they had to end it here and now, a part of her was screaming in protest. Her heart was being ripped into little pieces.

All that talk about protecting Timmy...well, she wasn't sure if it wasn't too late for that, too. Last night when she'd tucked Timmy in, he had included Ace in his nightly prayers. He had told her that he thought he would like Ace to read him a bedtime story the next evening. His favorite bedtime story that ordinarily only she was allowed to read.

Oh yes, little by little, Ace had crept into her life and her heart and now her child's heart, too. How could she forgive herself for that? She, who had been so careful for the past three years, had tossed caution aside, telling herself that she had good reason for letting Ace close.

"And now look what you've done," she whispered. She'd done the unthinkable. Plus, she knew that getting over Ace wouldn't be like getting over John. For John hadn't cared, he hadn't protected her, he hadn't brought joy to her life and her body and her heart. He hadn't made her child's world glow.

Ace had done all those things. But he had to go. She had known that all along.

He would be devastated if he thought that she was crying over him. He would think he was repeating Ford's mistake.

"So he won't know. I won't tell him, I won't let on. I'll pretend I don't care."

The first step in showing him just how much she didn't care was to send him away.

"But not to the Overton Apartments. Not there," she whispered.

There were a lot of nice places to stay in Mission Creek, and she was very good at getting people to do things on a moment's notice. She would find a nice apartment that would take Ace in for tonight or for this week if he liked.

Then things would start to get better. Surely they would. Once he was out of her home and out of her bed and out of her heart, she and Timmy would be fine. They'd be safe again.

"Probably shouldn't be here. Might get caught and taken in." Branson Hines mumbled to himself as he stared up at the clean lines of the hospital. She was in there somewhere. He wished he knew just where.

But the hospital security was difficult to breach. Even more difficult to get past than that watchdog that had taken to guarding Crystal.

He snorted. He wanted Crystal Bennett's world to collapse the way his Deena's had. No one had paid attention to Deena when she'd lost her baby, but they sure as shootin' would pay attention to Crystal when he destroyed her.

Then they'd see that they couldn't destroy Branson Hines.

The hospital security or the dark-haired watchdog?

He smiled to himself, running his tongue over his teeth. It wasn't even a choice, really.

Even watchdogs had to close their eyes now and then.

Thirteen

When Ace stepped through the doorway into Crystal's house that night, he knew that something was different. The pale blue-and-cream decor, the golden gleam of the wood floor still warmed him. The flowers in their vases, the candles in their stands still felt like Crystal. He realized he'd begun to think of this place not just as hers, but as a home, a home he'd been sharing. None of the objects in the room had changed, but something was different.

He didn't have to ask what it was, either, not with Crystal standing there in the dining-room doorway looking pale and lost and sad. This was really it, then. Goodbye.

He felt the cold swirl through him. Not just through his skin but also his soul.

"Is Timmy here?" he asked.

She shook her head. "I didn't want to scare him."

So there was to be no goodbye there. He nodded, even though he thought she was making a mistake. Not that it mattered. She was Timmy's mother. She got to choose. He didn't want to think about how it made him feel, not being able to say goodbye.

But Crystal bit her lip. She knew some of it. "He'll see you around town until you're ready to go. I thought it would be best if we made your goodbye to him more…gradual.''

"How gradual?'' This wasn't what he had planned. He meant to go. A clean-cut quick escape. The thought of seeing her from a distance, going back to being less than a lover, was agonizing, even though he knew she believed she was doing what was best.

But when she looked at him, he could see that she wasn't any surer than he was. "I don't know. I—I looked in the newspaper today. I found apartments, nice ones. I don't want you to have to go back to the Overton Apartments.''

He managed to find something that resembled a smile. "You know that I didn't stay there because I had to, but because I chose to.''

She took a deep breath. "I know that, and I know why. I suppose if you choose to do it again, I can't stop you.''

But it would be different now. He would be choosing to move from Crystal and Timmy's hospitality back to a building that was little better than a brothel. Everyone would know that.

"It would be an insult to you and Timmy,'' he said slowly.

She shook her head. "Timmy and I have faced worse insults. That's not it. I just…I know Nola Warburn. I liked her when we were younger. I don't now. The sheets aren't clean, the rooms aren't clean. It's not a healthy place for a person to live. There's no warmth.''

"You think I need warmth?'' He couldn't help smiling at her consternation.

"Yes," she said on a whisper. "Yes, I do. I chose the best places I could find. I circled them," she said, and her voice sounded thick. She was looking down, handing him the piece of newspaper.

He reached out and took it, trying to ignore the fact that she was visibly shaken by this moment.

But how could he ignore it? He might as well ignore his own need for air.

Ace stepped forward into her space. He slid his hands into her hair. He kissed her. Softly. Slowly. Achingly.

"You want me to go," he reminded her.

"Yes." She nodded hard, though he could hear the tears in her voice, see the tears in her eyes.

"I could stay awhile longer."

"No." She shook her head just as hard. "No. Go. Just…just go somewhere where you can be happy and safe and comfortable."

He sipped at the tears that fled the corners of her lovely eyes. "That's important to you?"

She looked directly into his eyes. "You've been so good to us."

It was the worst thing she could have said. Gratitude. That was what this was about.

"All right, then." He took the page from the newspaper with the addresses circled. "I'll come get my things when I find something."

But as he moved outside and got into his car, Ace couldn't help swearing beneath his breath. He hadn't meant to stay even this long. He certainly hadn't meant to leave Crystal's house and go searching for an apartment.

He wanted to be gone.

No, what he wanted was to march right back inside and make love to Crystal all night long. He wanted to turn those tears into soft cries of desire. He wanted to change who he was, who he'd been all his life, and be the kind of man who could change every bad thing that had happened in her life.

Most of all, he wanted to be a different kind of man. The very thought almost made him laugh. He'd spent his life running from being a wanna-be, but now here he was, still wanting the unattainable. If he stayed here, everyone would think that he wanted his share of the Carson pie. If he could, he would like to be able to give Crystal the kinds of things the Carson wives had. But no matter how you looked at it, he was always going to be the outsider Carson, even if it was only in his own mind. Crystal deserved to have a better life than that and a better man than he was.

She'd had enough hurt in her life. And being who and what he was, he couldn't promise not to hurt her again. Most likely he *would* hurt her again, even if it was unintentional.

Damn, but he wanted to leave right now. This long-term slow leaving was going to kill him. Knowing she was right across town was going to make him crazy.

He looked down at the newspaper.

She wanted him to live in one of these places. He put the car in gear and began to drive.

Hours later he was still driving. Then he was walking. It was getting dark now. People were already starting to turn in, and he hadn't looked at a single apartment.

"No point," he whispered.

He wanted to give her the gradual goodbye that she wanted. But he didn't trust himself to let go gradually and not hurt her or Timmy. So he had to make it fast, final, so the healing could begin. And he wanted their last memories to be good ones.

Turning on his heel, he strode to his car, climbed in and made his way back to Crystal's.

She opened the door to him.

He scowled. "You didn't even look to see who I was."

"I knew it was you," she said, her voice a hushed whisper.

"How did you know?"

"I just did." Crystal stared up at him. How could she tell him that his presence was like a living thing that called to her? She always knew when he was in a room. There'd been no question who was at the door.

"Did you...did you find a place to stay?"

He shook his head. "It won't be necessary."

Her brow furrowed. "I don't understand."

"I know. I wish I could explain better, but... You want me to slip out slowly, to fade away like a shadow until you forget I'm here. I'm afraid I can't do that. When I go, I want to be gone. For good. Forever. It's for the best. For everyone. I'm not doing Timmy any favor by lingering and it's just not my way. So when we end it, we end it here. Now. We make it final."

Crystal wasn't sure how she managed to conceal the lump of pain that rose in her throat. She'd known it had to end. She'd even told him she wanted it to. But knowing the best thing to do didn't necessarily make it the easiest.

Somehow she managed to continue to stare into those fierce blue eyes. Somehow she managed to find her voice.

"Tonight?" she asked.

"Yes." His voice was harsh.

"Timmy's here. He's sleeping." She motioned to his room at the end of the house.

"That's all right. I'll say goodbye to him in the morning."

She knew what he was suggesting. Even as pain lanced through her, desire was building. If he was to go, she wanted to touch him again, she wanted to take him inside her again.

"The last time," he said, as if reading her thoughts. "We'll say our farewells tonight."

"Do you think… Is that a good idea?" Much as she wanted him, she didn't want him berating himself in the morning for taking her to bed and then walking away. She didn't want to be the one regretting anything, either, especially not when she'd promised herself she'd never go down this road again. Making love with a man one night, watching him leave forever the next day.

"It's a hell of a bad idea," he said. Then he stepped inside, closed the door behind him, snaked his hand around her waist and drew her to him. "And

I don't give a damn. If you do, you tell me no now. While I can still stop.''

His flesh was warm against her own, his scent swirled around her. She opened her mouth.

He waited.

"Yes," she whispered. "Yes, one last time. One time to put an end to things."

But it wouldn't really put an end to things. She knew that. She loved him. If she didn't, she wouldn't be here, doing this. And because she loved him so, she was going to regret every minute of this night come morning, and come mornings many months from now.

But not tonight. Not yet. For tonight she would not regret a thing. She would brand herself upon him if she could, so that maybe someday he'd remember her, remember this moment. And feel a sense of home, a moment when he belonged to a woman who loved him.

Crystal rose on her toes. She slid her hands up Ace's chest, looped her arms around his neck. "Kiss me," she whispered against his lips. "Kiss me and make love with me one last time."

He groaned. He opened his mouth over hers. Heat and need rose within her as he devoured her, claimed her. He swung her up in his arms and entered the bedroom where she'd lain while he'd slept on the couch. He pushed the door closed behind them.

"This room is just like you," he said as he laid her down on the bed. "All business on the outside." He motioned to the stark walls and tasteful prints. "And all warm and glowing and creamy on the inside." He stroked the peaches-and-cream-and-cinnamon quilt, then planted his palms on either side of her waist as he braced himself above her.

She smiled up at him.

"Yes, do that, angel," he said, keeping his voice low so that he wouldn't wake Timmy. "Smile at me. I want to remember you smiling."

She understood. He didn't want this last time to be sad. Neither did she.

He lowered himself over her. He kissed her, tasted her, brushing his lips over hers again and again. She wrapped her arms around him.

He rolled with her, taking her weight onto him, leaving her gazing down at him. He reached up and with one quick movement undid the clasp that held her hair. It spilled over her shoulders, framing her face.

"This time you control it," he said. "You give what you want, you take what you want. It's all you, as much as you want and as deep as you desire."

She bent and kissed his jaw. "And what about you? What about what you want?" she asked.

She felt him smile against her skin. "With you it's all good, all beautiful. You're a lovely, giving woman."

"Well, then," she said, her hands shaking as she tried to appear confident without letting him know just how much this meant to her. "Then let me start like this."

She leaned down and kissed him, as she moved her hands inside the jacket he still wore.

He raised up slightly to give her better access, and

she slid the jacket down his arms and freed him. She pulled it from beneath him and tossed it aside. It landed in a corner of the room.

Ace raised a brow. "J.D. wouldn't be too thrilled at your cavalier treatment of his favorite formal wear."

She smiled at him. "J.D. isn't here."

"Good thing, too. If he saw you like this, I'd just have to kill him, and as you know, I'm not—"

"A violent man," she whispered. "Oh, I know that, Ace. You're not a violent man, but you're a very desirable man."

She bent and kissed him beneath his chin, popping open the top button on his white shirt. One by one she released the rest of the buttons, then slid her hands beneath the cloth and spread the edges. Warm, muscled skin lay beneath her fingertips. She moved one finger and he nearly jumped right off the bed.

Crystal raised her eyes to his. Tension radiated from him, and he held his jaw taut.

"Sorry, angel," he told her. "But you make it very difficult to lie still. I want to touch you badly."

"Touch me," she whispered.

"I want you to be in control," he reminded her. He laid his hand on her thigh as she knelt over him.

A long shudder slid through her. "Ace, I don't think either one of us is in control tonight."

"I don't want you to feel, come morning, that I took advantage of you." His eyes turned serious and dark.

She couldn't help smiling. She leaned forward,

dropping a light kiss on his chest. "I'm sitting on top of you, darlin'," she reminded him.

He smiled back. "My name's not darlin'," he said, handing her back some of the first words she'd said to him.

"Allow me to help you with this." She opened his shirt farther. "Your hands appear to be full." Another line from that first day.

He moved his hand farther up her thigh, making her gasp. "Only one of my hands is full," he told her. But then he slipped his other hand beneath her skirt and touched her inner thigh, stealing her very breath and thought and sanity.

"Both my hands are occupied. Now you can help me," he said, his voice low and thick.

And she somehow found his mouth with her own. She tunneled her fingers into his hair and kissed him like there was no tomorrow. Because there *would* be no tomorrow, she knew. They were back to the beginning in many ways, living old memories, the kinds of things people did when they knew they would never see each other again.

But not yet. Please not yet, she thought.

I love this man, right or wrong, foolish or not. The thought followed her as she pulled his shirt from him.

"Make love to me, Ace. Please," she said. "Help me." And so he helped her. Gently he undressed her. He kissed her, slid his skin over hers.

"I wanted you from the first," he told her. "Just like this." He coaxed her onto him and helped her lower herself until he was deep inside her. He urged her to take everything they both wanted.

She did. For long minutes she rocked with him, made love to him. "You wanted me like this?" Her voice was a broken cry.

"Yes. And like this," he whispered as he turned with her and drove into her depths. "I wanted you every way. All of you. Just as you are tonight."

His words made her ache, his hands made her gasp. She lay beneath him, cradling him inside her as the heat rose and she matched his rhythm, knowing that tonight she would travel to a place she'd never known before and would never know again.

She'd wanted him, too, that first day. And now he was here. "Have me," she whispered and she looked up at him as he linked his fingers with hers, pushed their hands up above her head and plunged into her, sending her senses whirling as the stars fell into her soul.

"Ace!" she cried, and he drank in the sound. He held her, waited for her, his body tense and deep inside her. Then he moved again, almost left her, then slid inside her once more as every muscle in his body stiffened. His head fell back in a silent shout. Her own body surprised her by shuddering once more in a slow and blissful release. She took Ace's weight and wrapped her arms around his back, holding him to her.

After what seemed like too short a time, he raised his head. "I'm crushing you, darlin'." He started to move to his side.

"Not yet," she whispered. He gazed down into her eyes, then relaxed against her.

"Not yet," he agreed, but she noticed that he

shifted slightly so that most of his weight was off her. He left one arm and leg entrapping her, claiming her.

She gently touched his cheek. He smiled. "Are you all right, sunshine?" he asked, his voice sleepy.

"Yes," she murmured, knowing she was. But she was also close to tears when she thought that come morning he would leave forever.

He stroked the sensitive skin at her waist. "Are you sure?" His voice sounded even closer to sliding into sleep.

In that moment she knew that she loved him beyond hope. Even tired as he was, he wouldn't allow himself to drift off without making sure she was all right, taken care of.

"I'm very sure," she said, kissing his hair. And she *was*. Very sure that she had fallen so deeply in love with Ace Carson that she would never stop loving him. He had come to town friendless, with revenge on his mind, but he had never stopped caring for people. For women and old people and small helpless children. He thought of himself as a man with few scruples, but he had more honor than any man she knew. And a great deal of pain. A past that wouldn't let him free.

She could love him, but she could never hurt him by asking him to tie himself to that past by staying here with her and Timmy. If he stayed, he'd have to stare his past in the face every day of his life.

And so she stroked his hair until he slept. She kissed his shoulder, tried to think what life would be like, how she would make a life for herself and

Timmy while they both loved a man who lived his life far from theirs.

Silent tears streaked into her hair, but she held herself still for fear of waking Ace. Slowly weariness claimed her. She slept, knowing that the morning would tear the fabric of her life. Knowing that she had willingly stepped right into that pain. And would do so again with no regrets.

Something woke Ace in the darkness. He glanced down to where Crystal lay beside him, tendrils of her long beautiful hair drifting across his shoulder, linking them. He raised himself on one elbow and gazed down at her. He fingered a bit of the silky stuff, kissed it with his lips, breathed in her unique scent, a scent that made him weak with need every time she got near. Moonlight filtered in through the window, silvering her features.

She'd been crying, he thought, his heart wrenching at the thought. Because she thought he'd used her like other men had?

He swore beneath his breath. Somehow he had to make her see that this was different, that he cared. But maybe Timmy's father had told her that, too. Maybe he wasn't so different from the men who had hurt her. After all, he had taken her sweetness, made love to her and said his farewells. Where was the difference?

She looked so small in the bed, so fragile, so sweet. He wanted to tuck her into his body and keep her safe. He wanted to slay monsters for her, to make her his, but he hadn't slain any monsters for her, had he? His own monsters were pulling him away.

He lay back down beside her. He listened to her breathing, willed his heart to beat in concert with hers. He wished things could be different. Wished he could have her and stay with her and love her. Forever.

But forever, he knew, was elusive. Forever was what his mother had wanted with Ford. She'd wanted family and had it snatched from her.

Crystal moved in her sleep and Ace lay quietly, just loving the business of watching her sleep. She had tried so hard to give him family. She had bent over backward to link him up with his brothers and sisters.

His throat nearly closed. There wasn't a reason in the world Crystal should care whether or not he patched things up with the Carsons. But she had cared. Because she was Crystal. So very special.

She was going to be a very difficult woman to leave. She was going to be impossible to forget. He dared to lean forward and breathe in deeply of her scent. Then he touched his lips to the sweet skin of her cheek one more time.

At last he rose and began to dress. Crystal stirred and he stopped, standing as silently as he could, unwilling to disturb her dreams. Finally her breathing fell soft and regular again. She rested her palm on her cheek like a child.

Ace's heart broke in two, but he continued dressing. He readied himself to leave so that he could make it fast when the time came. Fast, so his emotions wouldn't have time to betray him.

Somewhere in the house something shifted, squeaked, crashed. A sharp cry was cut off, muffled. A small thud came from the far bedroom.

Instantly, Ace raced to the door and out into the hall, his heart thundering. "Timmy! Are you okay, bud?" he called as he skidded to a stop just outside Timmy's bedroom and wrenched open the door.

Timmy didn't answer, but there in the moonlight was a man, his hand over Timmy's mouth, dragging him toward the window.

"Let him go." Ace couldn't see if the man had a weapon and he didn't want Timmy to get hurt, but there was no way he was going to let anyone take this child.

The man turned and snarled at Ace, and Ace saw that it was Branson Hines. But in that moment Hines yanked Timmy closer to the window.

The little boy's muffled whimper cut through to Ace's soul.

"This doesn't concern you," Hines said, his voice high and tight. "It concerns her and those like her. They killed my baby. They took my Deena's happiness. This time *I* take."

"Don't even think of leaving." Ace's voice was icy, crisp, commanding. It could have been his stepfather's school-principal voice, or Ford's cattle-king voice. Both powerful men. *He* needed to be powerful now.

He was watching Branson's hands, the man's eyes. His own gaze tracked every movement, looking for weakness. If he jumped Hines now, the man might still have time to hurt Timmy. The boy was so small, so helpless. His eyes were huge and scared above Branson's hand.

"Hey, wildcat," Ace mouthed. Somehow he managed to wink, even though this wasn't a winking matter. He wanted Timmy to think that he had things under control, that they were playing a game even if it wasn't true.

Just don't let him be so frightened. And give me strength and good timing. He sent the plea heavenward.

"Timmy had nothing to do with the loss of your baby," he said in that same commanding voice, edging slightly to the side, keeping Hines watching him, turning so that he was no longer in such a good position to leap for the window.

"It isn't fair that she has a son while I don't," Branson whined. "She was supposed to lose everything years ago. I planned it that way."

A small gasp sounded behind Ace, and he felt rather than saw Crystal behind him.

"Ace?" Her voice was a low quiver.

Branson smiled, and it was an ugly thing to behold.

"Oh, this is better. I hadn't planned it this way, but having her watch while I take him away is so much better."

Ace felt Crystal's pain and panic almost like a physical thing. It knifed through him. At Branson's first words she had started to move forward, but when the man jerked Timmy aside a bit, she'd stopped. Now Branson was leering, daring Crystal to do something.

Reaching back, Ace touched her hand gently.

"Branson seems to need to talk to you, darlin'," he said. "Get some things off his mind. Could take a few minutes." He hoped and prayed she understood the message he was trying to send her.

He heard her take a deep breath, as if preparing for battle.

"Close your eyes, Timmy, sweetheart," she said softly. "Think of riding Freckles and having cookies and milk with Grace. Think of how soft Bert's fur is and how you and Ace take care of him." She looked at Branson. "Mr. Hines and I are going to talk. Tell me about your son."

Her shift in tone from frightened to calm seemed to make Branson nervous. He glanced wild-eyed from side to side. He couldn't know what Ace knew, that Crystal was shaking. The hand he was touching trembled with fear.

Ace brought that hand to the small of his back. He gave it a gentle squeeze of reassurance before letting her go.

She took another deep breath.

"What do you care about my baby?" Branson practically screamed the words.

Ace shifted to the side as if to give Branson better access to her. He hated doing that, exposing her so, but his move had the expected effect. Branson pivoted to stare directly at her, a vein throbbing beneath the pale stringy hair at his temple.

"I care about all babies," Crystal said, and as Branson zeroed in on her voice in the waning moonlight, Ace slid farther to the side. He watched the grip that Branson had on Timmy.

"So why didn't you get your rich friends to save my Deena's baby?" Hines leaned toward Crystal.

Ace reached for Timmy's dresser and picked up the first thing he touched. Something hard, heavy.

"A woman has to take care of her body to have a healthy baby, Hines," Ace said carefully. "She has to make an effort. Maybe you should have told your wife that. Told her she needed to stop drinking, at least. Maybe you should have helped her."

Branson swung in his direction. "You—"

"Here," Ace called, tossing the item he'd picked up to Hines, praying that human nature still held for an animal like him.

The object sailed through the air. Branson obeyed the call of nature, reaching out to catch, and Ace dove for his legs.

"Run, wildcat," he ordered, and Timmy stumbled away just as Ace crashed into Branson, sending both men to the floor. Regaining his balance, Ace drew back his arm and drove his fist into Branson's face.

"If you ever touch anyone I love again, I'll knock you clear across the state of Texas. You come near my woman or my child again and I won't leave breath in your body. No one hurts Crystal or her boy. No one even breathes a bad word about them."

He lifted Branson as he spoke, shook him, and then shoved him back to the floor and held him there.

"Timmy?" he whispered. "You okay, bud?"

"Yes, Ace." The little voice was high and scared, and Ace dared to look away from Branson long enough to note that the boy was clinging to his mother.

Ace applied more pressure to Branson to hold him in place. "I'm sorry you had to go through this, Timmy, and had to see me lose my temper," Ace said, tears threatening to thicken his voice. "I'm normally not a violent man."

He looked over at Crystal and she was smiling at him, tears streaming down her face. "You're not," she agreed. "But we're glad that you were able to violate your principles tonight."

She held on to Timmy, but the look she was giving Ace... It was all he could do to keep holding Branson in place when he wanted to take her into his arms.

"Call the police," he told her.

"I did. When I first woke up and heard you. They should be here soon."

As if on cue, a siren sounded in the distance, growing louder by the second.

"We make a great team," he said as if he'd just discovered something.

"Me, too," Timmy said.

"Oh, yes, wildcat, especially you, too."

The sirens sounded in the street just outside the house. Ace looked toward the window and saw the streaks of daylight crisscrossing the sky.

"It's morning," he said quietly.

And he looked at Crystal.

Fourteen

After the police took Branson away, Ace simply stood there looking at Crystal and Timmy.

"What?" she asked softly, her arms around her son.

"Nothing." He shook his head. "It's just…the two of you together, it's a beautiful sight. You're a family."

Crystal gazed down at her son, who smiled up at her. She kissed the top of his head. "Yes, we are. We most certainly are, just as you and your mother were."

It was such a simple thought, but one whose truth had escaped him until that moment, the fact that he and his mother had been a real family. He'd always thought of them couched in the terms that other people tossed his way. Illegitimate. White trash. Dysfunctional. An abandoned woman and child. Even after his mother had married Derek, people still didn't look at them as a real family. No doubt they thought that Derek had done both him and his mother a favor. His stepfather hadn't been a demonstrative man, and so people hadn't been privy to the quiet love he'd reserved for Rebecca and her son. They'd made up their collective mind about Rebecca years earlier and, in the small community of the academy, nothing of any consequence had happened to change it.

Ace had been just as close-minded as everyone else.

"We *were* a family," he said, feeling something burst inside him. "But we didn't talk about that kind of thing. We never used the word family the way you do. The way you demonstrate its importance. All the time I *did* have a real and whole family, even though I didn't know it. Thank you for reminding me of that." He only wished he could have realized it while his mother was still alive.

Crystal's eyes were shining. She reached out and touched Ace's hand, then linked her fingers with his in the briefest of unions. "She knows." And he marveled that she could know his thoughts.

"You'd better go feed Bert," she told her son, giving him a pat on the behind. "He's going to want his breakfast soon."

"Yeah," Timmy said, his eyes round. "And he's going to want his rock, too. I better find it."

Crystal and Ace exchanged confused glances.

"His rock?" Ace asked.

"The one you throwed at that man. I been putting sticks and grass and rocks in with Bert. So it feels more like the outside. More like a home. That was Bert's rock, but it's okay if I can't find it again. You and me needed it more than he did."

"Yes, we did," Ace said, remembering his desperation when Branson Hines had threatened to steal Timmy away forever. "Tell Bert thank-you, and if you can't find his rock, I'll help you. Or we'll find another one.''

But as Timmy nodded and toddled off, Ace looked at Crystal and saw that her smile had disappeared. "Don't make promises to him you can't keep," she whispered. "It's morning."

Yes, morning. The day he was going away. Leaving Crystal. Leaving his heart. His family.

She'd wanted him to have a family, the one he'd thought he'd never had. She'd taught him that people in families that had been broken didn't have to live broken lives. They didn't have to be bound by the past or by a sense of injustice.

He'd spent his whole life wanting things he couldn't have and trying to hide this desperate desire. He hadn't wanted to be weak. He'd done his best to break free of needing anything or anyone.

But he knew without a doubt that he had never wanted or needed anything as badly as he wanted Crystal Bennett.

And he didn't care who knew his weakness.

Some things were more important than fear or anger or distrust or past injustices. Some things could make all those things look puny and insignificant in comparison. Things like love, hope, family.

All things that Crystal Bennett represented. Things she'd wanted him to have.

He smiled at her and moved closer, bringing his hand up to cup her neck. "It's a beautiful morning, isn't it, sunshine?" he asked.

Her eyes opened wide as he leaned close to taste

her. And then he was kissing her and her eyes were closed, her arms around him.

"Ace?" she asked, her voice shaking when he let her go. "What's wrong?"

He stroked his thumb over the velvet of her cheek. "Maybe you should ask me what's right."

She tipped her head, clearly confused. "Okay, what's right?"

"This." He dipped his head and kissed her lips softly, sweetly, swiftly. "You. Alive. Well. Healthy. This morning, when I stood there between you and Branson, and I thought he might take Timmy or hurt you, or both, I knew what it was to face losing everything important. All my life I thought I was missing something important, and maybe I was, but that something was something I'd never known, anyway. It was an illusion, a daydream, something that had become larger than life and not quite real, because of not having it and having had years to embellish it. But you and Timmy, you're real. This time I knew what I was going to lose, and it practically killed me to think of it. So yes, for this moment everything's right and beautiful. You're here, safe and alive and beside me."

She took a step closer, bringing herself up against him. Her cheek rested on his chest, her hands clutched the front of his shirt. She breathed in his scent and then turned her head, rose on her toes and touched her lips to his neck. "I was afraid, too," she admitted.

"Of course you were."

"No." Her fingers gripped the cotton of his shirt more tightly. "I don't mean just about Timmy or even myself. To tell the truth I didn't have time to think about myself. My mind was going crazy for Timmy, but somewhere deep inside I knew you weren't going to let Branson take him and I was afraid... Branson is crazed. I think he would have tried to kill you if you made him angry enough, and I've heard that anger can make a man strong. If he had hurt you..."

She let her words trail off. She gazed up at him, her eyes swimming with tears. Then she smiled. "I'm so happy you're much smarter than he is. I'm so very glad you came to town, Ace, and that I got the chance to know you."

"I want the chance to know you better." The ragged words felt as if they had been ripped from him involuntarily, as if he couldn't help saying them. "I want you to let me love you. I want you for my own, but..."

The look on her face was resigned. She'd heard that before, or something like it. From other men, ones who'd hurt her.

He shook his head, then said, "Don't look that way. I've never told you anything I didn't mean. I want the chance to know you better." Forever, he wanted to say, but he couldn't do that. Not yet. "I have a few things to take care of, though. Will you...will you wait?"

He hated to ask that of her. It wasn't fair when he wasn't even sure what he was planning.

She nodded tightly. "Where are you going?"

That was a very good question. He'd figure it out real soon, he hoped.

"I'm not leaving Mission Creek, if that's what you

mean," he whispered, giving her a quick hard kiss. "And I plan to be back before the sun is much higher in the sky if I'm lucky."

"And if you're not?"

He ran his hand lightly along her jaw. "If I'm not, look for me, anyway. I'll tell Timmy goodbye for now."

And then he turned and walked out the door when all he wanted to do was fold her into his arms and stay with her all morning.

Crystal watched Ace go, his back broad and strong, his stride long and full of purpose. Another man walking away from her, but he had asked her to wait.

Was there really any reason for him to stay? Any reason for her to believe that this time things would end the right way, the happy way?

Only that this man was Ace, not just any man.

Some people might say that the very fact that the man was Ace was reason enough not to trust him to return. Even he had been telling her for several weeks now that he was leaving. Even he had told her that he wasn't a man who wanted to fit in or have the things most people wanted.

Yet the memory of his risking his life for Timmy and her filled her up. The catch in his voice when he'd said he wanted to get to know her better wouldn't let her go. Not that it mattered whether waiting for him or believing him was right or wrong. She loved him completely, without rhyme or reason or end, and nothing was going to change that. Not even Ace.

She waited. She put the house in order. She cleaned up Timmy and she put on her nicest dress, a pearl-colored sheath. Then she did what women have done through the ages. She stood at the window and waited for the man who held her heart.

When he finally drove up, it was all she could do not to run out the door and throw herself into his arms.

As it was, he had barely knocked on the door before she opened it.

She had expected him to smile, expected him to tease or to kiss her. Instead, he stood there looking as if he was going to a hanging.

"Ace?"

"Nerves," he said. "I've…I've set things in motion that can't be taken back." He took her hand, started to lead her out the door. Then he stopped. He cupped one hand around the back of her neck and kissed her long and hard. "For courage," he told her. "Would you go get Timmy? We're going for a ride."

She did as he asked, but when they exited her house, she noticed that the car in the drive wasn't the one he'd been driving lately.

"You stopped at work?" she asked.

He nodded. "Yes, but this isn't a Mission Creek. It's a Lone Star."

When he turned onto the road that led to Carson Ranch, she stared at him.

"No promises," he said. "No idea what's going to happen, either. I called all of them and asked if this was okay. All except Ford."

She didn't have to ask what he was doing. She

didn't exactly know, but it didn't matter. He was doing something.

"This has to be for you, Ace," she whispered, touching his sleeve.

He glanced at her. "It is, in part. It's also for us."

"I don't need you to do this if it's too hard."

He looked at her again and gave her a sad smile. "I need to do this, and everything that matters is probably hard."

She smiled at him then. He took one hand off the wheel and touched her hand. She took it and kissed his fingers, then she drew a breath.

"I love you, Ace," she said simply.

The car nearly swerved off the road and missed the turnoff for Carson Ranch. Ace grabbed the wheel with both hands, made the turn and drove slowly down the drive, pulling to a stop in front of the massive house.

Then he turned to her, leaned over and kissed her full on the lips. "What in the world did I ever do to deserve you in my life? You are the most amazing woman, Crystal Bennett. I was a fool to ever think that I could spend even one day with you and not love you. When this is over—" he looked at the massive house "—well, it's just not going to be over. Not between you and me. Not by a long shot, darlin'."

Her heart filled. It overflowed. "I love when you call me darlin'," she said.

He turned to her then, one brow raised.

She shrugged. "I didn't want you to know, because it affects me so much, but I shiver when you say it. But only when *you* say it. Only you."

He kissed her slowly, reverently. And then he kissed her again. "We're going to have a lot of talking to do real soon, darlin'. And a lot of kissing, too."

With that, he climbed from the car and moved around to the other side to help her and Timmy out.

"I'll hold you to that," she said as hope began to build in her heart. She looked at Ace and saw that he was staring at her as if he wanted to devour her, but then he looked at the house again.

And everything hopeful in his face froze.

"Let's get this done," he said.

She followed him up to the door. There was, she knew, a lot riding on what happened in this house. Ace was a proud man. He wouldn't take a woman to wife if he considered himself a failure.

If anyone beyond these doors made him feel that way, she was going to tear them limb from limb, Carson or no Carson.

Crystal moved close to Ace's side and tucked her hand against his side.

Two minutes later Ace stepped over the threshold of the Carson family home for the first time. The room was richly furnished, open, airy, large, befitting a family as old and wealthy and powerful as the Carsons. But none of that mattered. What mattered was the row of Carsons facing him. The ones he'd called. And the woman and child at his side.

He looked down at Crystal, straight into those trusting hazel eyes. Just looking at her gave him strength, made him feel taller.

"Maybe Timmy would like something to eat," he

suggested, and looked at Grace. Within seconds the older woman had hugged Timmy and called the housekeeper, who took the little boy into the kitchen.

Ace waited until he knew Timmy was gone and busy. Then he took a deep breath and looked straight into Flynt's eyes. And then into Matt's, Fiona's, Cara's, Grace's. One by one he acknowledged each.

They waited. A bit nervously, it seemed to him. Which was ridiculous, of course. They weren't the ones who'd been thickheaded. *He* was. He was the one who had to try to make things right.

"I just wanted to tell all of you a few things that I need to get off my chest," he began slowly. "You may have heard this already, but early this morning a man came into Crystal's house and tried to take Timmy away. He tried to hurt him and Crystal, and I learned a few important things in that moment. I learned that maybe the past doesn't matter much if you have a future. I...well, I decided that I want to have a future. Here in Mission Creek. No more looking backward, no more placing blame, no running from the good things that have been staring me in the face, the people who've reached out to me."

He made the mistake of looking at Grace just then, saw the tear tracking down her cheek, and his throat filled. He swallowed hard. He looked up at the ceiling, praying for the strength to go on without breaking down, and hoping for the words to convey what he needed them to know. "I can't tell you— What I mean is, Branson Hines tried to take the two people I value most in the world, the woman and child I love. The sheriff tells me Hines is most likely going to the maximum-security prison in Lubbock. Real soon, too. I'm glad he's going to be off the streets. The women and children of this town can be safe now. I guess what I'm saying is that I've come to think of this town as my…my home.''

Blindly he reached out. Crystal caught his fingers and held on. He raised her hand to his lips and kissed it. He loved that he could do that, reach out for her and have her be there. Just touching her hand felt right. It balanced him and helped him to continue.

Ace looked up then and stared straight into Matt's eyes.

"You don't have to do this, big brother," Matt said.

Ace contemplated that for a moment. "No, you're wrong about that. I need to do this, and I want to. You're all a part of this town. You've gone out of your way for me, done more than I had any right to expect. I gave you grief and yet you held out your hands. That means a lot to me. So I want you to know that this morning I bought a piece of land just outside town. It's the first bit of land I've ever owned or wanted to own. So I guess I wanted you to know that I'm planning on staying in Mission Creek. After the way I've behaved to all of you, I realize that it might be a problem for the Carsons having me here. I've done my best to embarrass you and to steal your family's business. That was unworthy. I apologize for that. And I apologize for being so ungracious when you offered me hospitality. I only hope that…'' He cleared his throat and swallowed. He tried looking at Fiona and saw that she was leaning forward as if hanging on his every word. Cara was smiling at him as if he'd never done anything wrong. Matt and Flynt were actually starting to grin.

Ace took a deep breath. "I hope that you'll find a way to forgive me someday," he continued haltingly. He cleared his throat again. "I just wanted to let you know that I intend to keep a lower profile from here on out. I owe you that much. And I want to thank you for allowing me to come to your home to say these things and for giving me the chance to—"

But he didn't get the chance to say another word. Grace suddenly rushed toward him and threw her arms around him. "You don't owe us a thing. Not a thing. We're just so glad you're here. At last. At last you've come home," she said, and Ace's eyes filled with tears. He didn't hesitate; he wrapped his arms around her, too.

"I'm not even related to you. Not really," he said, his voice breaking.

"Who says you're not? Just let anyone try." She turned toward her children with a warning glance.

Ace looked up and saw that Flynt and Matt were grinning broadly now, Fiona, too. Cara was looking a bit misty-eyed.

"Ma's always right, you know, Ace," Fiona said. "Don't even try to argue. Just...welcome home, big brother." Then Matt and Flynt were pounding him on the back, and Cara was hugging him and all of them were making plans to find him a room at the ranch now that he was staying.

Amidst all this, footsteps sounded in the next room.

Ace looked up and saw his father waiting in the doorway. Like a stranger. An outsider.

Glancing down at Crystal, Ace gazed into her eyes and saw a woman who didn't care if he sold cars or dug ditches or owned oil wells. She didn't care if he knew who his parents were or not. He saw a woman who loved him, a woman he would love for eternity, and he gathered strength just from looking at her. Then he stepped away until he was standing on his own.

"I thought you should know that I'm planning on staying in Mission Creek," he told Ford. "But I wanted you to know that I'm not doing this to make you uncomfortable or to exact some kind of revenge. I'm staying because—" his glance strayed to Crystal again and he smiled "—because I've found something important here. So I hope it doesn't disturb you to know that I'll be living my life in the same town as you. I'll do my best to stay clear of you if that's what you want. I'm done with living in the past. You hurt my mother, but maybe she wouldn't have found my stepfather if things hadn't happened as they had. I wouldn't have known him. They wouldn't have shared a wonderful love. I wouldn't have all these brothers and sisters who come in and buy cars they don't need," he said, grinning at his half siblings. "I guess what I'm saying is that I don't know what would have happened if you'd stayed with her, but I'm through wondering and wanting things that can't be, and regretting. I just wanted to let you know that I'll be around." Then he gathered all his courage;

he risked everything he'd always thought he could never risk.

He stepped forward and held out his hand to the man who'd given him life.

Ford didn't respond.

As Ace started to draw back his hand, he looked up into his father's eyes. Tears were streaming down Ford's face.

"Don't." Ace had wanted the word to come out gently, but it was a harsh cry.

Ford shook his head. "When I saw you that day with your stepfather, I knew what a poor excuse for a man I'd been. You were a boy any man would have been proud to call son, and I'd thrown that away. I'm not saying that Rebecca and I should have wed. I didn't love her, and it would have been unkind to pretend otherwise, but I could have done right by her in other ways. I could have at least acknowledged and taken responsibility for our child. Knowing that, I felt...I felt I didn't deserve to step in and be your father when I'd let so many years slip away. You had a father who loved you. Injecting myself into your life then seemed wrong at the time, but that was a mistake, I think. I've regretted it for years. I've made mistake after mistake where you're concerned. I'm going to spend my life regretting every one of them."

Ace managed to shake his head. "No, don't. It's time to stop regretting. It's time to make a start."

This time Ace didn't wait for his father's handshake. He put his arms around Ford and hugged him. When he let go, he wasn't sure which tears were Ford's and which were his.

"What made you come around?" Fiona asked, and Ace smiled.

"You."

His little sister looked confused. "Me?"

"Yeah. Weren't you the one who kept throwing me at Crystal every time I turned around? Weren't you the wise woman who knew that I was going to fall in love with her if I spent just fifteen minutes talking to her?"

He turned to Crystal and took her hands in both of his.

"I love this woman so much," he said, "that I'm going to spend every day of the rest of my life thanking God for making me pigheaded enough to come to Mission Creek to get revenge on the Carsons. I love this woman so much that I could kiss you, little sister, for choosing her for me."

Crystal crossed her arms. "I'll have you know that I'm a grown woman, Ace Carson."

He raised a brow. "Which means?"

"I do my own choosing. We're just lucky I chose you to love."

Ace looked at her then with such a gleam in his eye that Crystal's heart seemed to leap to her throat. How could she have ever fought loving this man? She was so happy that he was going to stay in Mission Creek. But as she gazed into his eyes, he dropped to one knee before her.

"You know what my staying means, don't you?" he asked.

Her heart started hammering, and her blood heated.

She felt the rest of the room spin away as if they were the only two people there.

"Tell me what it means," she whispered.

"It means that I want you for my wife. I would be the happiest of men, the luckiest man on earth, if you would agree to marry me."

She smiled at him.

"And to love me."

"You know that I love you beyond belief," she said. "I couldn't stop loving you if I tried. And I did try hard not to love you."

He took her hand, turned it over and placed a searing kiss on her palm. "Thank goodness you didn't succeed."

"What woman could fail to love you?"

He chuckled at that. "Any number of them, I imagine, darlin', but I'm so very glad that you're not just any woman."

"No, I'm not. I'm your woman."

"And you'll let me make Timmy my son? Would you do that?"

Crystal felt tears come to her eyes. "He already is, Ace. He already loves you, talks of nothing and no one else when you're away."

"Mmm, that's good," he said, kissing her fingertips, one by one. "But you still haven't answered my first question. You told me once that you didn't want a husband." His voice was slightly unsteady, slightly edgy. She knew then that telling him she loved him wasn't enough. No doubt many women had told him they loved him over the years. He'd never, though, she'd wager, loved a woman enough to ask her to marry him.

The very thought that he loved her that much brought her to her knees. She sank down beside him, facing him.

"I can't wait to be your wife," she whispered.

"We won't wait long," he promised. He slipped his hands around her waist and pulled her to him, kissing her warmly, deeply, repeatedly.

Someone cleared his throat and Crystal raised her head. She grinned at Ace. Together they turned and saw that all the Carsons were smiling.

"I hope you'll let me bestow a wedding gift on you," Ford said. "You're a Carson, you know."

But Ace shook his head. "I'm happy to be a Carson, but I don't want my son being told that his father came to town to claim his share of the family wealth."

"No one would dare to tell my grandson that, and Timmy will be my grandson," Ford said sternly.

Still Ace hesitated.

"Taking my money makes you uncomfortable, doesn't it?" Ford asked, his voice laced with sadness.

Ace shook his head. "It's not that. It's just—I've lived my whole life feeling that I had to make my own way. I'm not sure that I can change that, or that I want to."

Ford smiled. "All right, then. I won't be hurt if you won't take my money. You're a man for a father to be proud of. Will you at least let me will your share to Timmy and whatever other children you and Crystal might have?"

"Gladly," Ace said, his voice breaking slightly.

"That's fine. That's so good. Looks like our family just got bigger and better, Grace." Ford beamed at his wife and smiled at all of his children who were looking just as satisfied as he was. "Looks like everything's settled."

Ace shifted from one foot to another. "Not quite everything. There is one more thing I wanted to talk to you about."

Ford waited.

"About Lone Star Auto. I thought you might be in need of a good salesman."

The Carson brothers and sisters whooped, but Ford smiled proudly at his oldest son.

"My boy, you're a lifesaver," he said. "I was beginning to think I was going to have to close the place down, but if I could get you to manage it, I think we might save it."

"I might have a few ideas," Ace agreed, smiling at his father. "We'll talk about it later, but now, I hope all of you don't mind, but I'd like to be alone with Crystal."

He and Crystal went into the next room, where Timmy was playing with a piece of dough the housekeeper had provided. "I heard you was going to be my daddy," Timmy said, smiling at Ace.

"I would love to be your daddy if you'll have me, wildcat," Ace said, kneeling by the little boy.

"I'll have you forever," Timmy said, and he wrapped his little arms around Ace's neck and hugged tight. "Now I'm going to make a family," he said, picking up his dough. "You go with Mommy. She's going to cry. Happy tears, like me sometimes.'' He smiled again.

Ace kissed him on the cheek and stood. He turned and took Crystal's hand.

''Aw, hell, darlin', I want you much closer than that,'' he said, swinging her up into his arms and striding away, gazing into her eyes all the way.

''Don't you think you should have a wedding before you get that look in your eye, son?'' Ford asked.

''As soon as possible,'' Ace said, kissing Crystal.

''We'll start the plans once we're alone,'' Crystal agreed, kissing him back.

But as Ace kicked the door open and walked across the porch carrying his bride-to-be, he heard Flynt laugh. ''You sure you're going to plan a wedding tonight, big brother?''

''Absolutely,'' he said, kissing Crystal.

''Positively, my love,'' she said, kissing him twice.

''We're just going to plan it real slow.'' And the last Carson brother gathered his bride-to-be close to his heart, where she was a perfect fit.

* * * * *

You will love the next story from Silhouette's
LONE STAR COUNTRY CLUB:
MISSION CREEK MOTHER-TO-BE
by Elizabeth Harbison

Available September 2002

*Turn the page for an excerpt from this
exciting romance!*

One

"...Branson Hines escaped from authorities while being transferred from Mission Creek to a high-security prison in Lubbock. The thirty-two-year-old Hines is described as five foot ten, with dark eyes, dark blond hair, and an unkempt goatee. Police spokesman Darryl Reilly warns that Hines is volatile and may be armed."

Melanie Tourbier reached out and clicked off the radio of her rented convertible. Then she shuddered and tried to take a deep cleansing breath as her yoga teacher in London had instructed. If things were going to work out the way she wanted them to here in Mission Creek, she needed to relax, to think positive thoughts.

Her cell phone rang on the seat next to her, and she punched the "on" button, glad for the distraction.

She slipped the hands-free earpiece into her ear. "Hello?"

"Where *are* you?"

Melanie smiled at the sound of the voice. It was her friend Jeff. "I'm in Texas," she said.

"Melanie Tourbier, you must be crazy!"

"I've made up my mind and I'm going through with this." She readjusted her grip on the steering wheel, symbolically reconfirming her resolution. "Face it, pal, you're going to be an honorary uncle."

"Much as I'd love that, I think you're going about this the wrong way," Jeff argued. "You've got plenty of time to meet a man the traditional way, not in a test tube."

"Oh, Jeff, don't be silly. They don't keep men in test tubes here," she teased.

"They keep the *essence* of them there, and don't change the subject."

"I've already tried men."

"One bad husband doesn't mean that there's no one good out there."

Melanie laughed. "Maybe not, but it certainly opened my eyes to some of the bad that's out there."

Melanie had decided she was through with romance. She still, however, wanted a family of her own. So she'd done some research and learned that the fertility clinic at Mission Creek Memorial Hospital was one of the best in the world. As well as one of the most discreet.

"So what are you going to do?" Jeff wanted to know.

"I'm going to meet with a family-planning counselor," she said. "A Dr. Cross. Doesn't he sound nice? As I understand it, I have a quick chat with him, assure him that I know what I'm doing, and then *bingo,* I'm off for the procedure. Or at least the first one." She smiled at the thought. "Who knows? Next time you hear from me, I might be pregnant!" She hung up the phone and returned her full attention to the road before her, literally and metaphorically.

A couple of minutes later, she pulled the car into the parking lot, took a ticket and found a spot right in front of the door. She was feeling lucky.

She went inside and strode straight to the elevator, pressing the button with a flourish. "One step closer," she said excitedly under her breath.

"I beg your pardon?"

Startled, she whirled to see a man standing there. He was tall and dark, with the most striking pale green eyes she'd ever seen. "I...I was just talking to myself."

"Oh. Sorry, didn't mean to eavesdrop."

She smiled. "I guess someone who's talking to herself has to accept eavesdroppers as part of the deal and hope none of them are psychiatrists."

He gave a strange smile. She immediately thought her joke was idiotic and now he probably thought she was, too.

His eyes were mesmerizing, like a hypnotist's watch. She couldn't look away.

He was looking at her, too, and he frowned slightly, as if trying to place her. "I'm sorry, do we know each other?"

"No, no. I don't think so. But you do look...familiar," she finished lamely. He didn't look familiar at all. This was not a face she would have forgotten.

The bell dinged behind her and she heard the elevator doors open. She turned and walked into the mirrored car, conscious not so much of the thirty Melanies that seemed to step on with her, but of the thirty tall, dark-haired, green-eyed strangers.

She reached out to press the eighth-floor button at the same time he did on the opposite side of the door. She glanced at him and said, with a nervous little laugh, "Popular floor."

He smiled.

When the elevator lurched to a stop, Melanie, who'd pulled her wallet from her bag to retrieve her appointment card, dropped the compact leather case at the man's feet. She reached for it at the precise moment he did, and they bumped heads just as the elevator doors opened.

"Sorry," Melanie said, her embarrassment increasing by the moment.

He laughed and handed her the wallet, which had ended up in his hand like the big end of a wishbone. His fingertips brushed hers. "Nice bumping into you." He gave an attractive grin.

She groaned at the pun as they both stepped off the elevator. She took out her wallet again to retrieve the appointment card.

Melanie watched him go, vaguely hoping she might meet him again. Something about him was interesting, reassuring. She shrugged the notion off and looked closely at Dr. Cross's business card. Suite 818. She put the card back into her bag and followed the signs.

Minutes later Melanie was sitting in the waiting room of Dr. Jared Cross's office, trying to ignore the continuing radio coverage of Branson Hines's escape. The announcer repeated warnings that citizens may be in danger, then returned to the Muzak program.

"Miss Tourbier?"

Melanie jumped, even though the voice was soft. "Yes?" She looked at the petite redheaded receptionist who'd called her name.

"The doctor will see you now." The receptionist gestured toward the door next to her desk.

Melanie gathered her things and gave a brief smile. "Thank you."

She entered Dr. Cross's office.

He was standing with his back to her, facing a wide shelf that was overflowing with books. She couldn't tell much about him from behind except that he was very tall, and his hair was as black as a raven's, or at least it seemed so in contrast to the generic white doctor's coat he wore. His hair color and his physique suggested that he was much younger than she had expected.

"Dr. Cross?"

He turned quickly. "I'm sorry," he said, flashing an apologetic smile.

It was the man from the elevator.

SILHOUETTE *Romance*

Escape to a place where a kiss is still a kiss...
Feel the breathless connection...
Fall in love as though it were
the very first time...
Experience the power of love!

Come to where favorite authors—such as
**Diana Palmer, Stella Bagwell,
Marie Ferrarella** and many more—
deliver heart-warming romance and genuine
emotion, time after time after time....

Silhouette Romance—
stories straight from the heart!

Silhouette®
Where love comes alive™

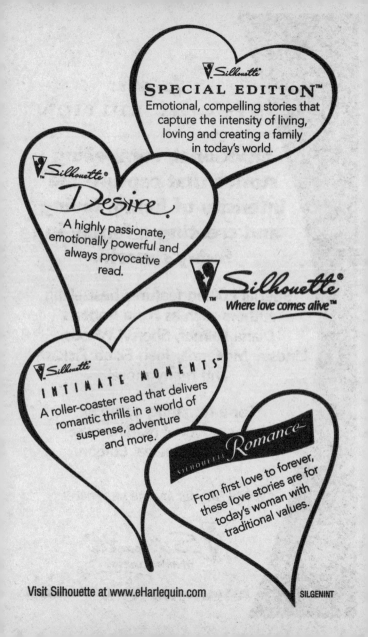

Silhouette

SPECIAL EDITION™

Emotional, compelling stories that capture the intensity of living, loving and creating a family in today's world.

Silhouette®

Desire

A highly passionate, emotionally powerful and always provocative read.

Silhouette®

Where love comes alive™

Silhouette

INTIMATE MOMENTS™

A roller-coaster read that delivers romantic thrills in a world of suspense, adventure and more.

SILHOUETTE Romance

From first love to forever, these love stories are for today's woman with traditional values.

Visit Silhouette at www.eHarlequin.com

SILGENINT